STEAMING

A SEA STORY

MARK DAVID ALBERTSON

Irish Viking
publishing

ALSO BY MARK DAVID ALBERTSON

Spying: A Sea Story (2021)

Stalking: A Sea Story (2022)

For my shipmates

ACKNOWLEDGMENTS

Any novel is a combined work of many people. Many thanks to my supportive shipmates, friends for life, even though we might have lost touch over the years. Thanks go out to my parents, who had the will not only to let me go but to encourage me to join the navy when I was a mere seventeen years old.

Thanks to my editors, Edmund Pickett and Karen Meuir who challenged my ego and forced me to rethink what I was writing and how it made sense to readers. I'm not saying I'm a great writer, but every great writer has great editors.

Most of all, thanks to the love of my life, Karen FitzGerald Meuir, without whom my novel would have remained in the dusty shelves of my mind.

PREFACE

Preface to the Second Edition

This was my first novel, and as with all things, one's first attempt at anything is likely to be less polished than succeeding endeavors. Nevertheless, much as I was tempted to edit and embellish the second edition, I left it the same as the first. Hopefully a reader new to my writing will forgive my tenderfoot novel and give others a try. That being said, this book was a labor of love and had been in my head for over 45 years before its completion. This *was* my first rodeo, and hopefully my successive books will each improve.

Mark David Albertson, October 2021

The only difference between a fairy tale and a sea story is that a fairy tale begins, "Once upon a time," and a sea story starts, "Now this is a no shitter ..."

—B. S. Boggs, SMC, USN

Now, this is a no-shitter ...

THE LOUD DARKNESS

Darkness and noise. The figure dressed in green camouflage fatigues sat on a thick branch of a large tree as far from the ground as he could possibly climb. In front of his eyes was the blackest night he had ever seen. Not one single speck of light shone anywhere. He couldn't see his hand in front of his face, and he was deep in the jungle, many miles from the nearest source of light. In complete contrast to the darkness was the hammering noise surrounding him; the noise of the jungle was louder than anything he had ever heard, louder than an urban street at rush hour. From no direction and all directions came animal noises—birds, monkeys, unidentifiable growls, and imagined demons. Imagination was, in fact, his worst enemy. As he listened to the cacophony of the jungle, his mind spawned images of gorillas, tigers, pythons, and a variety of terrifying beasts, all focused on making him their banquet.

This was the second night he had spent in a tree. His mission was only advanced during the day. There was no point to even trying at night. There was also no point in trying to sleep. Even though being on the ground during the day was fear-provoking, the night was a terrifying, waking nightmare that allowed not one moment of slumber.

He tried to focus on his mission. He had two nights and three days to reach his goal. The goal was approximately five miles from where he had entered the jungle: a rendezvous point where, if he reached it in the time allotted, he would find a helicopter and a team to extract him from this bit of hell. In the meantime, he had a canteen of water, a survival knife, ten feet of fishing line for snares, five matches, a compass, and a survival saw. He had no weapons, no rain gear, and no radio.

He tried to calm his anxiety and terrified trembling and focus on planning for the mission. The plan was simple: survive, and make it to the rendezvous point. Both were equally important, yet his empty belly dictated his priorities. He had been in the jungle alone for a day and a half—more important, for two nights—and had found no food. Snares failed, and the animals tended to be just beyond his ability to find. He remembered his training, which included what the instructors called the rule of threes: a person can survive three minutes without air, three days without water, and three weeks without food. Fortunately, water had been easy to find, as it had rained almost continuously for the entire time he had been in the jungle. In fact, he was completely soaked from head to toe, and his feet felt as though they had been in a lukewarm bathtub for a week. His body told him, however, that he needed to find food. That, unfortunately, would have to wait for morning light. In the meantime, in an attempt to distract himself from his dark imaginings, he found himself thinking about the twists and turns in his life that had brought him to this moment.

His recollection started with a vision of an exceedingly large haze-gray Chevy van lumbering through the gates of Naval Station Pearl Harbor, each seat filled with an excited and anxious young man. The two sharply dressed, perfectly postured, and unsmiling marines waved the driver through the gate, and as the van rolled past, the vaguest sneer came over the face of one of the guards.

1

HAZE GRAY

As Seaman Matthew Bertram sat in the rear seat of the navy van, he marveled at the crisp blue uniforms and serious looks the gate guards wore. Matt had been told once by his boot camp company commander that the marines had been guarding the gates of naval bases for two hundred years, and they hadn't lost one yet. They had apparently honed their gate-guarding craft very well. He assumed the marines completely resented this characterization.

As the van entered the base, Matt wondered how he had gotten all the way from the small town of Los Alamos, New Mexico, to the incredibly exotic island of Oahu. He had been born and raised just a few miles from the Los Alamos Scientific Laboratory. His parents were both employees of the once-secret research facility that designed and built the atomic bombs that annihilated Hiroshima and Nagasaki and effectively ended the war with Japan, along with the lives of over 100,000 Japanese people. Growing up in that city would have been a strange experience for almost anyone. His birth certificate listed his official place of birth as Post Office Box 1663, Santa Fe, New Mexico; the city was still a secret. Everyone's address was that same post office box in Santa Fe, which seemed to Matt to have been a pretty big clue to potential spies that something fishy was happening in the area. The school system in Los Alamos County was funded by the federal government, and the government provided an education that the town with the most PhDs per capita of any city in the world would demand. Matt would say that he was the product of the finest private school on earth, paid for by the taxpayers of the United States. Everyone's father was Doctor This or Doctor That, winner of the Fermi Prize, the Nobel Prize for Physics, and any other prize that nuclear physicists would covet. The city had an amazing social stratum, which was based upon position at "the lab." Matt's parents were, unfortunately, not scientists, and his family was, therefore, something akin to the skilled craftsman caste in the Middle Ages. They were part of the massive support staff that made sure that the lab ran smoothly.

Matt's classmates were just as incredible as their parents would expect. Fully 20 percent of his high school class graduated with 4.0 grade point averages, which made choosing a class valedictorian a conundrum. Unlike most of his classmates, Matt's interests were in the subjects of art, shop, graphic arts, and, even more unlikely, typing classes. Typing in and of itself was not particularly important, but Mrs. Whipple, the typing teacher, was, in Matt's opinion, absolutely the most splendidly gorgeous woman who ever walked the planet and was the subject of his pervasive adolescent sexual fantasies. Matt had taken every class Mrs. Whipple taught, occasionally twice, including typing 102, 103, 104, and 105; several accounting classes; and, naturally, the secretarial curriculum, and he was the only male student in the Future Secretaries of America Club, for which Mrs. Whipple was faculty advisor. For Matt, it was well worth the hazing from his classmates and the incredible provocation he endured from his basketball team—*well* worth it, if only to attend the club and watch Mrs. Whipple and her amazingly ample breasts.

The science club at Los Alamos High School was the largest club in the school, but Matt's senior yearbook review of participation listed only the Ski Club and the Future Secretaries Club. Besides fantasizing about cuddling with Mrs. Whipple, skiing and shooting were Matt's passions, and he took every opportunity to do as much of both as he was able. While some of Matt's classmates cut class to smoke pot or drink, Matt cut class to ski in the winter and shoot bottles and cans with his twenty-two in the spring.

Matt loved the outdoors. He had been camping and backpacking since he was very young, and nothing made him happier than having a fishing pole or his twenty-two in his hands. Matt and his best friend, Mike, spent three afternoons a week when the weather was good at an old abandoned pumice mine, shooting their twenty-twos. Matt would often shoot two or three hundred rounds with the old Remington rifle that his grandfather had given him when he was twelve, and he had gotten pretty good a slaying pop bottles and beer cans.

As Matt's senior year in high school rolled around, his laughable class standing made graduating with his class of 1974 a reach. Matt's low GPA forced him to give careful consideration to what options he would have following graduation. His schedule the last year of school contained a list of the best classes for an easy A. Additionally, Matt's father made the decision very easy for Matt.

"Son," Matt's father said to him one evening during his senior year, with his most *father-knows-best* face on, "we need to discuss what you will do after high school."

Matt realized in an instant that his fate was somehow sealed, without much input.

"I need you to know, Matt, that I haven't saved any money for your college education, so if you want to go to college, you'll need to find a way to pay for it yourself."

That was *not* good news. Matt's other friends were busily planning four (or maybe five or six) years of partying on their parents' dime at fashionable Ivy League colleges in the East or at least Stanford. In truth, Matt couldn't stand the thought of going to college, but he had a keen interest in attending the University of Colorado because there were no fewer than seven ski resorts within an hour's drive. Since he had resigned himself to the depressing reality that Mrs. Whipple would be very resistant to his moving in with her, college seemed like the next-best option, so he worked hard on getting good grades in photography and auto mechanics in order to graduate on time with a GPA high enough to get into the University of Colorado.

"So," Matt's father went on, "I want you to know that if you want to get a job, you can live with us for three or four months after graduating, if you pay us rent for your room." Additional bad news. The word *job* sounded like a terrible idea, and the word *rent* was even worse. And because Matt's professional career thus far had been mowing lawns and being a lifeguard at the local pool in the summer (a good gig, by the way), a decent job seemed a bit out of reach.

"Or ..." Oh wow, there was a third option? The first two really sucked, so Matt was hoping that the third option would be something within the realm of tolerability. With that word, Matt's father pulled out a glossy, full-color recruiting brochure from the US Navy. On the front was the tagline, "It's not a job ... it's an adventure!" The flashy brochure was filled with pictures of very happy sailors doing sailor jobs and looking very adventurous.

Matt quickly calculated the opportunity, and his sense was this might be the best option. He could go on an "adventure." He wasn't aware of any naval bases near ski areas, but it didn't involve rent, jobs, or college. Matt was instantly sold. He would join the US Navy. That was his choice. Matt chose adventure! Given the fact that the draft was still on and college education deferments were being eliminated, everything seemed to point toward volunteering to go on this adventure that some called "The Navy."

The next day, Matt jumped in his prized 1963 Dodge Dart and drove to Santa Fe to the navy recruiting office. Chief Petty Officer Max Garcia greeted Matt at the door with a navy Frisbee, a ruler, and a bumper sticker, all of which were reciting Matt's new mantra: "It's not a job; it's an adventure!" Matt was given a "Navy Job Aptitude Test" (the NJAT ... the first of *many* acronyms Matt would come to know), and CPO Garcia told Matt he scored well enough to do any job in the book. With that incredible offer, he handed Matt an actual book of navy jobs. Within this magnificent catalog was a veritable plethora of fascinating-sounding jobs. Matt instantly saw one he liked: photographer's mate. Matt had taken several photography classes in high school to bring his GPA up to something that allowed him to graduate, and from what little he remembered, it was pretty darn easy. "That's the one!" Matt excitedly stated.

"Oh, I'm sorry, Matt," Chief Garcia said, "that job's closed. Since the Vietnam War is pretty much over, we are cutting a lot of jobs, and that's one."

Undaunted, Matt found another: heavy equipment operator with the Seabees. The job sounded pretty cool. Once again, Chief Garcia gave Matt a sad face with a subtle shake of the head and said that job was closed also. With more study and focus, Matt narrowed his choices down to the one job that looked the most exciting: boatswain's mate. That job sounded like the best. The book described the boatswain's mate as the "master seaman" and "jack of all trades."

"Harrr!" Matt said. "That sounds like the best job ever!" Matt imagined himself climbing the sail lines to the crow's nest, looking for land, and shouting, "Thar she blows!" or "Land *ho!*"

"That one's not closed, is it?" Matt asked the chief. "I like the idea of climbing the sail lines to the crow's nest and shouting, *'Land ho!'*"

Chief Garcia stared at him for a moment with a look that seemed to signify that he didn't think Matt was the sharpest tool in the shed.

"No, Matt, that job is not closed, but that's really a job for people who are mildly retarded or who can't read," Chief Garcia mumbled. "It's mostly chipping paint, painting, and chipping more paint. And when you aren't doing that, you are scrubbing dirty walls, hauling food aboard ship, and standing lookout outside in rain, wind, and sleet. Boatswain's mates haven't shouted 'Land ho,' climbed lines, or spotted land from crow's nests in the last, oh, 150 years or so. You did good on your test. How about being a radioman?" he asked. "This is a great job, no heavy lifting or paint-chipping, and you get to work in an air-conditioned space!"

Well, if Matt couldn't be a boatswain's mate, he guessed air-conditioning was the next best thing. Matt signed the contract, and after physicals and oaths, he was given a date to report for boot camp just after his high school graduation. With the benefit of nineteen seconds of thought, Matt was now going to be a navy radioman.

Matt's first ride in a navy van had been in the one that delivered him to the Naval Recruit Training Center, San Diego, for boot camp. After a two-day train ride from Albuquerque, Matt was finally at boot camp. His only real memory of those first moments was complete and utter fright. As he exited the van at RTC San Diego, he saw all around him young men with no hair, facedown on hot asphalt, doing push-ups, with loud, scary men screaming obscenities at them. Matt had not actually ever heard such astonishing strings of unending profanity as were targeted at these poor recruits.

Much like in the movies Matt had watched with boot-camp scenes, upon his arrival, there were the stereotypical drill instructors shrieking at the recruits, as Matt and the others disembarked the van that had brought them to Navy Recruit Training Center, San Diego. The first thing those who greeted the van did was to point to a series of twenty-five phone booths and inform the new recruits they needed to call home and let their families know they had arrived safely and that they probably wouldn't be hearing from them again for about six or seven weeks. Matt's phone call went something like this:

"Hi, Dad. It's Matt."

"Matt, did you arrive safely?"

"Yes, Dad. Dad? There are a bunch of people being mean to a bunch of people with no hair."

"Yes, Son. That's boot camp."

"Dad?"

"Yes, Son."

"I've changed my mind. Air-conditioning is not worth this."

"Sorry, Son, it's too late. Let us know when you graduate from boot camp."

"Yes, Dad."

Matt's mother would confess years later that each day Matt was away at boot camp, she expected to see him appear on the front porch, AWOL. Since Matt had quit everything he had ever signed up for in his young life, it was a reasonable assumption that boot camp would be a task far beyond his ability to complete successfully. Fortunately for Matt, the navy was not in the habit of allowing its new recruits to quit just because they changed their minds. Had this not been their policy, the navy would have had a force significantly smaller than they needed to accomplish their mission, which most certainly would not have included Matt. After thirteen weeks of push-ups, verbal abuse, marching, running, calling everyone with a uniform "sir" regardless of rank, and gradually becoming absorbed into the collective called the US Navy, somehow, Matt made it to graduation, went to radioman school, and did so well that he was also sent to teletype repair school. With his new skills, Matt headed to Pearl Harbor to meet his new home, the USS *Robert E. Peckham*, FF-1099.

The navy van was in the process of making its way down a very long pier next to the harbor, dropping sailors at the gangplanks of their new ships. Tied up to the pier were mammoth gray warships, including destroyers, cruisers, tenders, and supply ships. It was difficult to imagine that this was the same pier that was there in 1941, in which battleships and destroyers were demolished in the attack by the Japanese. To Matt, the ships looked like a great, giant parade of hulking elephants, tied head to tail, larger than anything he had ever imagined. Each had lights on the stacks, the sides, and the bows. Each made amazing whirring noises as generators pumped water and fed electricity to the haze-gray behemoths. To Matt, the scene before his eyes felt like the Las Vegas Strip, as he observed the lights, noises, and activity on the ships. He strained to see where his ship was. Matt had done a bit of reading prior to arriving in Pearl Harbor and discovered that the USS *Peckham* was a Knox-class fast-frigate, named after some explorer who had led an exploration mission to Antarctica and had died there in the cold, along with twenty-three people dumb enough to accompany him, mostly due to the fact that he had neglected to bring sufficient food on the journey. The *Peckham*'s mission was twofold: antisubmarine warfare and escorting aircraft carriers on deployment. These mighty ships used to be called destroyer escorts, but somewhere along the line, "fast frigates" sounded oh so much more romantic, harkening back to the warships of the seventeenth and eighteenth centuries, so they were redesignated by some committee of admirals who didn't have anything more productive to do.

The van had gradually emptied at each stop along the pier until it was just the driver and Matt. As it came to a stop at the last ship on the pier, the huge numbers painted on the bow of the ship appeared: 1099. That was his ship! As the driver opened the rear and side doors and Matt grabbed his sea bag, suddenly an intense anxiety arose in his gut. In boot camp, the recruits had been schooled on a formal protocol of entering and leaving a ship, traditions dating back to well before people kept dates. Matt hoped that his boot-camp lectures would come in handy now. As he struggled to remember the protocol, Matt wished he had paid more attention.

As the van drove away from the gangplank of the *Peckham*, Matt stood, sea bag over his shoulder, paperwork in his hands, and proud to have three small diagonal stripes on his dress blues. Matt had signed up for the "delayed entry" program, a gambit created by some genius in recruiting for the navy. Under this program, the navy would allow seniors in high school, with their parents' permission, to join the navy up to a year prior to graduation. In exchange, they were able to get one higher rank upon completion of boot camp. This allowed the navy to have a large group of contractually committed recruits in the pipeline, long before they were truly able to make a responsible decision about their futures. Because of this, Matt spent minimal time as a "seaman apprentice," and by the time he had completed radioman school, he was an E-3 seaman, which meant better pay, even though he still knew pretty much nothing about being a sailor. Yet Matt, standing in front of his new home, erroneously felt like the *Old Man of the Sea*. No more cadences like, "Looky over there, that recruit ain't got no hair." Matt was experienced. He thought, standing there in what the public regards as a proper sailor uniform, lovingly called "Cracker Jacks," with the kerchief, white hat, and backflap, about to board his navy ship, that he was downright salty. He uttered a quick "harr" and headed for the gangplank. Matt, believing he was a seasoned sailor, had been in the navy all of five months, and his pores oozed navy, or so he thought.

He took a deep breath and walked up the gangplank to the quarterdeck of the ship. Despite five whole months in the navy, this was Matt's first experience onboard a "real" ship. There was a chief petty officer on quarterdeck watch, and he stood by to engage in the traditional ceremony of coming onboard a naval warship. Matt saluted the flag on the fantail and then saluted the chief and said, "Can I come onboard the ship?" Unfortunately, that was not even within the realm of the required ritual. Matt had apparently somehow gotten it wrong.

"Perfuckingmission denied, sailor!" the almost jovial chief shouted with a big smile on his face.

Now what do I do? Matt thought. He had somehow not spoken the right words. Matt stopped on the gangplank, which was not terribly stable, wobbly with the waves in the harbor, and thought.

"Permission to come on the ship, *sir!*" he said.

"Fucking perfuckingmission denied," said the chief, "and I ain't no goddamfucking, sir ... My parents were married, asshole!" decried the chief. He was obviously enjoying the encounter with this unversed idiot.

Matt was stuck. Two *fuckings* in one sentence could not be good. Matt couldn't remember what to say, and now he was flustered, fearing he was forever condemned to standing on a gangplank. Those hours of lectures in boot camp about Captain's Mast, courts-martial, and the Uniform Code of Military Justice came rushing back, and Matt feared he'd be hauled away to the brig because he couldn't report for duty. Several extraordinarily long minutes passed, as Matt stood uncomfortably at the bottom of the gangplank, futilely searching for those magic words that would allow him access to the ship. He came up completely empty. The chief gave Matt no help. He simply stood on the quarterdeck, staring at Matt with his arms folded.

Forlornly, Matt stood, head down, trying to dig for the proper words that would unlock the door to his new ship. Nothing came to mind. He was about to give up and surrender to a life of hard labor in

a navy prison when, out of the darkness, he heard singing and swearing. Two inebriated sailors appeared in the light, arms around one
another's shoulders, staggering and swaying as they sang some sort of
drinking song. They approached Matt, pushed him aside, and said to
the chief, in slurring speech, "Perfuckingmission to come aboard?"

They apparently were granted permission by the surly officer of
the deck! Matt's visions of bread and water disappeared, and with
glee, he seized the moment and decided *that* was the key language.
He debated for a moment whether the word *fucking* was the necessary password to gaining access. He decided at the last minute that
the "fucking" part was optional, so he left it out. Voila! Matt was given
permission to come aboard. The chief looked at Matt's orders with
deep concentration for what seemed like an eternity. Finally, he
looked at Matt and said the following incomprehensible statement:
"Oh, you're a fucking Twidget. That's OC." He told a sailor standing
next to him to "call below" and get another "fucking Twidget" to
come up. The quarterdeck watch went to a small room right by the
gangplank, cranked a lever on a phone, and called someone, apparently "below." Matt assumed this all boded well, and even though he
had no idea what the chief said or what in the world a "Twidget"
could be, he decided it was a good idea just to go with whatever
happened. And if he was, indeed, a Twidget, at least one of his own
would come rescue him from this horrifying situation.

THE BOB E. CHICKEN

A dmiral Ira Stevens had been the youngest man to serve as the chief of naval operations, known as a "CNO" in the navy. It is the top job in the navy; the CNO is the supreme boss of the US Navy. Ira entered naval service in 1942, in the middle of World War II, and served until 1976. He was one of the longest-serving CNOs in the US Navy's two-hundred-year history. Other than his incredibly bushy owl-like eyebrows, Ira was best known for his dream of putting his mark on the navy when he took over: to make the navy the "new" navy. Ira felt that the "old" navy was not representative of the technology, arms, and manpower of the modern navy, and it was time to look and act differently than the navy had since it had been established in 1775 by the first Continental Congress. Ordinarily, the person sitting in the job of CNO had little impact on the rank and file. Although Ira made many changes while he was CNO, there were two prominent changes that most sailors of the day remembered and that directly impacted Matt. The first was allowing sailors to grow beards, just like the sailors of old. This was a very popular, albeit mostly unattractive, change, as the majority of those who chose to grow beards were between eighteen and twenty-two, a time in which many, if not *most*, young men grow some sort of patchy, scraggly growth that barely passes for what most think of as a beard. The second change was incredibly unpopular. Ira decided that the navy uniform should grow up and become something more sophisticated than the traditional sailor uniform of "Cracker Jacks" and the traditional white "Dixie cup" hats, something that to this day people still think of when they picture a sailor's uniform. Apparently, Ira did not consult anyone who had to wear the new uniforms, and the changes were met with keen resistance. Unfortunately, Matt was caught in the middle of this transition. Early in boot camp, he was issued the "old" uniform of traditional sailor attire, and ten weeks into boot camp, he was issued the "new" uniform, which looked completely unlike anything anyone would expect sailors to be dressed in. The dress blues included a double-breasted, dark, almost-black suit, and the Dixie cup hat was traded for a traditional brimmed hat, much like police, airline pilots, and milkmen wore. Most sailors who had been issued the new uniform wore it with some embarrassment. The public didn't recognize it, and many sailors recall being accosted by passengers in airports asking if they were the pilot of the plane (if in dress blues) or a milkman (if in dress whites). Rarely could anyone outside of the navy identify the new sailors as actual sailors.

One other change of Ira's that would directly affect Matt was his creation of the "landing force deployment team," which met with unanimous opposition by the Joint Chiefs of Staff but which Ira fought for to the bitter end. This concept would have the most significant impact on Matt's life, but at this point in his tenure, the uniform debacle required some amazing effort, as Matt discovered, requiring him to carry two full sets of different uniforms with him to his new home, the USS *Robert E. Peckham*.

The first half of the 1970s was a difficult time for the navy as well as for a country highly divided over a "conflict" many thousands of miles from home. Despite one's opinion on the virtues or vanity of the war in Southeast Asia, after nearly 60,000 soldiers, sailors, airmen, and marines had been killed in action and over 150,000 wounded in action and some 1,600 were missing in action, practically everyone in the United States, from the president to Jane Fonda, was very weary and looking to find a way to get out of Vietnam with some semblance of honor. The navy's role in Southeast Asia had been multifaceted; riverboats had patrolled the rivers and provided air- and ship-based artillery support (a.k.a., bombing), aircraft carriers served as mobile runways for navy fighters, and navy destroyers lobbed artillery shells on the Viet Cong to support ground troops, while at the same time, navy hospital ships provided care and comfort to those wounded on the battlefields of Vietnam and Cambodia. Yet, Vietnam was absolutely winding down. Almost everyone in the United States had become exhausted by the conflict, and yet thousands of soldiers, marines, and airmen were still stationed "in country." Even as the American public was told that Vietnam was practically over, a much less public war was taking place in Indochina, outside of the eyes of the American media and the public. Much of this unpublicized war would not be disclosed outside of military circles until many years later.

Little of that mattered to Matt at that moment. As he stood waiting for what seemed like hours on the fantail of the ship for another "Twidget" to show up, he drank in the newness of his experience. Gray up, gray down. Everything was gray. On the rear side of the ship was a room with some unnamed sailor on duty, calling on what was known as a "sound-powered" phone to various points on the ship and a chief petty officer in apparent command of the entire ship, or at least the entrance. It also quickly became evident to Matt that one could not speak a sentence or even a multisyllabic word without interposing the essential word *fuck*.

And then, a friendly face appeared. A very heavy man with one of those twenty-two-year-old scraggly almost-beards suddenly materialized from some dungeon underneath the ship. "Hey," the pleasant, plump man poignantly stated, "welcome to the *Bob E. Chicken*. I'm Pigman, and I'm here to get you settled in."

"I'm Matt!" Matt exclaimed, suddenly comforted by being with someone who was friendly.

Pigman put his finger to his mouth with the universal "shhh" signal and quietly whispered, "When the Wonder says who you are, you are that person. I'd prefer not to know what they called you 'pre-*Bob E*."

Matt had no idea who the Wonder was or what he would do, but he just wasn't willing to risk further opportunities to display his ignorance.

Pigman led on, and Matt followed with great trepidation, as the maze to wherever they were headed was considerable. All around him, apparently gray was the color of choice, with the exceptions of some walls, which were a sort of pea-green color. Through a water-tight door, down a stairway, along a passage, up a stairway, down a stairway, they went. It all just simply appeared to be the same, only weirder with each turn. There were pipes everywhere, coming in and out of the walls, and bales of wires running on the ceilings. The ship had obviously been created by someone much shorter than Pigman. At about six and a half feet, Pigman constantly had to duck under wiring, pipes, and doorways. Motors, vents, and whirring noises broadcast in every direction. Matt felt like the proverbial Alice down in some strange rabbit hole, and none of it made sense. As they descended into the gray metal bowels of the ship, Matt had a bit of momentary panic, wondering if he would ever find his way to fresh air again. It was absolutely incomprehensible to him that this maze of hallways, stairs, hatches, and wires could lead anywhere that anyone would ever be able to survive. After descending a final steep staircase into an abyss marked by the sign, "Operations Berthing," Matt was in his new bedroom, a "berthing" compartment with bunk beds stacked three-high, the width of the ship, housing fifty-five of the two hundred sailors on the ship. This would be Matt's new home. Pigman led Matt to the very back of the compartment. On a bottom bunk sat a very solemn man.

"Hey, Fuck ..." There was that word again, apparently used in a multitudinous context.

"I am Wonder. My real name is Steve Wundar, but here everybody calls me the Wonder."

Oh my god! Matt's wry sense of humor took over. *Stevie Wonder made it to the navy and is now sitting next to me. To make this internal* comedy dialogue even more entertaining to Matt, Stevie Wonder was a chubby white guy with a Texas accent and another one of those scraggly beards that appeared to be ubiquitous on this ship.

"Pardon me, Mr. Wonder," Matt mused. "I don't mean to be disrespectful or anything, but you just don't look like I expected you would look like if I ever saw you in person." Gutsy, yes, but in a quickly calculated move, Matt suspected, with all of Stevie Wonder's girth, he could outrun this guy.

Silence followed by more silence and then a laugh. "Fuck you, man. Of course, I'm not *that* Stevie Wonder," the chubby white guy said, "but I'm as close as you'll get, and I'm in charge around here!"

With that, it was settled. Matt had Stevie Wonder (a white guy from Texas) who was now in charge of his most immediate future.

Matt was shaken quickly out of his memories as a loud crash sounded on the ground below the tree he was in. His gut jumped into his throat as he heard another crash, and not fifteen feet from his perch in the tree was scratching and a low, guttural growl. Matt held his breath and struggled to keep his body as motionless as possible, hoping whatever it was would move on, quickly, without further trouble. He realized that whatever was there was actually at the base of the tree he was sitting in, and it didn't seem as though it was moving on. Matt risked taking a slow breath and hoped that the deafening sound in his ears of his heart rapidly beating was a sound only he could hear.

3

MANNY

First Lieutenant Emmanuel Kirschoff had been in the US Marine Corps since 1971. "Manny," as his friends called him, was a congenial young man, full of ambition and energy. When Manny enrolled at Dartmouth, his goal was to eventually go to medical school and practice medicine in his hometown of Wichita, Kansas. Manny had the grades and pedigree to attend any Ivy League college, yet he chose to attend Dartmouth mostly because his father and grandfather had matriculated from "Big Green." He found himself completely at home in the university atmosphere. He loved everything about college and especially Dartmouth, and coming from a good family, he pledged with Sigma Alpha Epsilon and settled into his studies. Manny quickly found that he had a passion for history. As a premed major, he was required to minimize history in favor of math and science classes, yet he found himself neglecting the required classes for history, public policy, and political science. His father had mixed feelings about those choices, but then, there could always be an alternative career path of law school and politics for his son, and as such, he acquiesced to Manny's choices. Manny had chosen Dartmouth partly because it came with a lacrosse scholarship, which had lasted exactly three games when he tore his rotator cuff in a match against Yale.

Manny joined ROTC at Dartmouth, mostly out of necessity. Although his family provided some support for college, his father had a philosophy that requiring his son to carry a substantial portion of the financial burden would help him to take college seriously, and it would mold him into an independent person. When Manny's scholarship evaporated, he found himself struggling to carry his share of the obligation. He needed money to finish his bachelor's degree, as Dartmouth was far from inexpensive, and there weren't many sources of funds to fulfill his share of the college burden. If he couldn't come up with the money for the next semester, his student draft deferment would end, and he was sure to be drafted. Having some college was just the same as no college to the government, which meant he would go into the army as a private, and it was a foregone conclusion that he would end up in Vietnam. With those odds against him, Manny joined the Navy ROTC and pledged as a Marine Corps officer.

ROTC was interesting for Manny, although he never considered himself much of a warrior. Having been an athlete, he enjoyed the physical conditioning and discipline, and the classes in warcraft had enough historical foundations to keep him interested and even compel him to excel.

The best part of ROTC, however, was that his college costs were covered by the government. The four-year obligation to serve in the marines seemed like a good trade to Manny, and with that, he finished college on the government's dime with a degree in political science and enough math and science to keep his medical school option open. Eighteen days after graduation, Manny reported for duty as a Marine Corps second lieutenant.

Once Manny had his orders, he accepted them without fail. The nature of Manny's personality was to accept life's circumstances, and he not only accepted his fate, he embraced it. Within three months of graduation from Dartmouth, Manny was on his way to Southeast Asia.

Manny's first assignment was command of a platoon in Vietnam, and he served three months in Indochina. While he was very inexperienced, Manny relied upon his sergeants to provide the knowledge and support he needed to command a platoon, even if he was completely in over his head. That tactic not only saved his life and the lives of his platoon members, but it created a good bond with his sergeants, and Manny quickly became known as an officer who knew what his job was. As Manny's combat experience grew, so did his confidence in the skills of a career marine. After three months in the jungles of Vietnam, Manny was fully expecting to be required to serve another three months before rotating home, and, if others' stories were accurate, he could expect another tour in Vietnam before his commitment was completed.

Much to Manny's surprise, however, the marines did not require him to finish his tour in Vietnam. The war was winding down, and the marines were already starting to reduce forces. Instead of going Stateside, however, the marines assigned him as platoon commander of thirty-six marines, along with a small air force contingent, to the Island of Mūc Ong, about sixty miles off the coast of Cambodia. While his command was small, he was assisted by three sergeants, Gunnery Sergeant James "Huck" Huckins, Staff Sergeants Wiley "Coyote" Engleman, and Thaddeus "Pop" Poplin. The platoon's mission was to secure the island as a strategic outpost in the event the US military needed a land-based operations center. Manny's platoon of marines and air force security police members landed safely with no incident and promptly set up base on Mūc Ong.

Mūc Ong, which means "squid" in Khmer, was a pleasant enough place. At just about one mile long and a half-mile wide, from a military perspective, it was not difficult to set perimeters, watches, and communications. The island had two natural coves, one to the east and one to the west, both difficult to see from the open ocean and deep enough to land swift boats. There were pleasant beaches on the eastern side of the island, and it was lush with palm trees and vegetation, which made camouflage a simpler task. The island could easily have been the site of a beach resort, which made being deployed there a less burdensome life.

Gunnery Sergeant Huckins, effectively second in command of the platoon, was an immense man, standing nearly six feet six inches and boasting twenty-two-inch biceps and a fifty-two-inch chest. His off-duty passion was martial arts, and he seemed to have little interest in anything that wasn't camouflaged or a weapon—or, even better, a camouflaged weapon. Despite his appearance, he was considered fair, if a bit abrupt, by his men, and he lived by the philosophy that he would never order any of his men to do anything he would not do himself. Huck was complex in his simplicity. He often told others, "There are three kinds of people in this world: ones you follow, ones you care for, and bad people." Although he was considered fair, he was also intolerant of languor and had a variety of methods to keep his marines squared-away.

Unlike Huck, the other sergeants in the platoon, Coyote and Pop, held a more distant feeling for the military. Although each was entirely competent, neither considered the marines his career (unlike Huck), and both were "short-timers" meaning their obligations with the marines would be ending soon. This led to an occasional conflict with Huck, who lived, ate, and breathed "Semper fi."

With a peaceful base established, Manny proceeded to post sentries, watch commands, and forward intelligence, just as he had been ordered, and he and his company of marines hunkered down to see if they were needed any further.

Life on Squid Island during those first few weeks was pacific, and it was not long before the marines let their guard down. Manny quickly discovered that he and his company had been, if not neglected, as least put on a very low priority, as the marine command was highly focused on extracting twenty thousand marines and all their equipment from Vietnam. Without the watchful eye of superiors, life gradually became more and more relaxed. Friday-night parties, impromptu volleyball tournaments on the beach, and barbeques marked their time on Squid Island. While Manny was careful to maintain some semblance of traditional marine discipline, it became an easy life much too quickly, and the small platoon was all but ignored by the command officers in charge of their company. Although they remained diligent, the combat platoon in Vietnam with its stress was gradually replaced by a group of young men enjoying the sunshine, beaches, and coconut palms of a very pleasant island in Southeast Asia.

Manny was the only commissioned officer in the platoon. This was rather unusual but was the result of an "incident" with what was supposed to be his second in command getting drunk on liberty and fondling the wife of the company commander, which left Manny without a second officer. Since militaries have existed, there has been a common rule that requires a line of distance between officers and enlisted personnel. This has always been for good cause. It is so much more difficult to order your "friends" into combat than the men you lead, and as such, ordinarily, officers and enlisted were not allowed to fraternize. But because it was more than a bit lonely all by himself, Manny decided to fudge just a bit on this rule. As such, Manny, Huck, Coyote, and Pop bunked together and became fast friends. As Manny had less actual battle experience and he had three sergeants who had significant combat experience and immense lead-ership experience, he was completely dependent upon his platoon and rifle squad sergeants on Squid Island.

While the fraternization rule was the first to go, many other rules were soon forgotten or set aside on Squid Island. The weather was extremely hot, and with no combat in their foreseeable future, the uniform of the day gradually became shorts, T-shirts, and flip-flops, with Mondays being the only full uniform day, just to prove they were still marines and not beachcombers. Even so, life felt much more like an island vacation. Although they were airlifted food and medical supplies on a regular basis, Squid Island yielded a wonderful variety of fish, both from the ocean and from a large stream that flowed near their base. The men regularly feasted on black shark minnow, golden carp, and catfish. Fruits were also plentiful, including bananas, dragon fruit, mangos, and more. Several of the marines created their own little wine-making business with a large glass bottle, grape juice, and yeast, capped with a condom to know when it had completed fermentation. They dubbed it "Squid juice," and the bar was always open for happy hour. With little to do each day other than swim, eat, nap, and drink, the once sharp-edged marines were quickly becoming more than a little bit listless, much to Gunnery Sergeant Huckins's dismay.

The command staff were not the only ones who had forgotten the company of marines. The Cambodians apparently had also, and because they were on an island off the mainland, the marines rarely saw anything to become concerned about. To Manny, this was the best of all possible options—no danger, no oversight, and a well-supplied base on a tropical island. As could be expected, however, the Cambodian government was beginning to realize there were still uninvited American troops on Cambodian soil, which was to provide an opportunity to expose and embarrass the American government in the worst possible way.

Being a fairly passionate student of history and politics, Manny was aware of the tumult taking place not just in Vietnam but in much of Indochina. He knew that in 1973 and 1974, the US government was motivated by a great desire to buy some precious time to withdraw, as quietly as possible, from the Indochinese Peninsula and, if possible, to protect its allies in South Vietnam. In very small part, the government also would have liked to prevent the spread of Communism to Cambodia, but truthfully, the United States just wanted to get the hell out of there. In addition to the Vietnam War, which most people remember, there were concurrent military operations in Laos and Cambodia, which most people *don't* remember. During the Vietnam conflict, and after five years of savage fighting, the Republican government in Cambodia, which was largely ignored by the United States.

The continuing conflict in Indochina was part of what became known among historians as the "Second" Indochina War, which lasted sixteen years and consumed the neighboring Kingdoms of Laos, South Vietnam, and North Vietnam.

For most Americans, and the federal government of the United

States of America, the Vietnam conflict officially ended on May 15, 1975, upon the US government issuing an official statement that the Vietnam conflict was over, just like that. Yet, despite the government proclaiming it done, outside involvement continued unabated, surreptitiously in Laos and Cambodia. US forces, including the CIA, continued to operate clandestine operations well after the 1975 declaration. In addition to several other operations, completely off the radar of practically every American because of an intense veil of secrecy by the US government, on a very small island off the coast of Cambodia, called Mūc Ong, the war continued for this group of US Marines.

Both Laos and Cambodia had many similarities with Vietnam. Most of their native populations were Buddhist peasants who lived poor but peaceful lives as farmers. Both were French colonies from the late 1800s, though colonial rule there was not as oppressive and socially disruptive as in Vietnam. Both were occupied by the Japanese in World War II and their local kings permitted to remain as puppet rulers. Laos gained full independence from France in 1953, when it was promised French and US military and financial support. By this stage, Laos also had its own Communist insurgency, called Pathet Lao, made up mostly of Laotians who had fought with the Viet Minh. By the late 1950s, a large area of eastern Laos was controlled by the Pathet Lao, along with North Vietnamese who had crossed the border to lend support.

To the south, Cambodia was led by Norodom Sihanouk, a charismatic young prince with a taste for Western culture, particularly Elvis Presley. Sihanouk was not short on ego: he produced his own films, organized public processions and parades (usually with himself at the center), and gave long, rambling speeches on Cambodian radio. But Sihanouk was also a progressive and a fervent nationalist who loved his country and wanted the best for its people. When the French granted Cambodia independence, also in 1953, Sihanouk took the radical step of abdicating as king and re-entering politics as a democratic candidate. He was immediately, and completely unsurprisingly, elected prime minister. Sihanouk was initially pro-American, but as US military action in Vietnam escalated in 1965, he adopted a more neutralist position.

In March 1970, Lon Nol led a successful coup against Sihanouk while he was out of the country. One of the new leader's first steps was to contact Hanoi and demand the withdrawal of all North Vietnamese Army (NVA) and Viet Cong forces from Cambodia. Not only was his demand ignored, but the North Vietnamese attacked Cambodian government troops, causing significant casualties. The Khmer Rouge, growing in number but still militarily weak, supported these North Vietnamese offensives. A massive "secret" US bombing campaign from 1970 to 1973 dropped 2.75 million tons of explosives on Cambodia, arguably the largest number of bombs dropped on any single country in history. This bombing killed thousands of Khmer Rouge, NVA, and Viet Cong—but it also alienated many Cambodians, who then joined the Khmer Rouge. By 1974, the revitalized Khmer Rouge was drawing closer to victory against Lon Nol and his forces. The group was now under the autocratic control of Saloth Sar (or Pol Pot, as most know him), a French-educated radical Marxist, who wanted to destroy the old institutions of Cambodia, so they could be built anew.

In April 1975, the Khmer Rouge seized control of Phnom Penh and the national government. Millions of Cambodians were frog-marched out of Phnom Penh and other cities, which the Khmer Rouge called "hives of bourgeois corruption." These displaced civilians were put to work in the fields and forced to labor from dawn to dusk without adequate food, rest, or medical care. Books were burned; money was destroyed; and communication infrastructure like television, radio, and telephone wires were all dismantled.

Much to the consternation of those "in the know," the conflict in Indochina was not over in 1974. More than a year later, Americans were still fighting and dying on Vietnamese soil. By 1975, the conflict in Vietnam had stopped, but fighting was continuing in other Southeast Asian countries, as a direct result of the American action in Viet Nam. The last "official" combat of the Vietnam War took place and is well-known as the "Mayaguez" incident. As the city of Phnom Pen in

Cambodia fell to the Khmer Rouge, they simultaneously captured control of all of Cambodia from the residual Khmer Republic forces. When Saigon fell on April 30, 1975, the Khmer forced all the Vietnamese forces to leave their base areas in Cambodia. The Vietnamese forces refused to leave a few areas that they claimed were Vietnamese territory and also moved to take control of several strategic islands off the coast of Cambodia, which resulted in several battles with the People's Army of Vietnam in the Gulf of Thailand and the South China Sea. Cambodia had a long history of claiming a wide area of territorial waters off of its coast. They had claimed twelve nautical miles of territorial waters for about six years previously and had regularly boarded ships on this basis. As of 1975, in direct disagreement with the Cambodians, the United States only recognized three nautical miles of territorial waters.

As part of these island battles, the Khmer Navy was very active in patrolling Cambodian coastal waters to thwart the Vietnamese forces and to control merchant shipping. The CIA was rumored to be using merchant ships to spy on the Cambodians, which, in fact, proved true. The Cambodians responded by capturing several fishing boats and smaller merchant ships.

On May 12, 1975, the US container ship SS *Mayaguez* passed by Cambodia. In US reports, the *Mayaguez* was about six nautical miles out, but evidence suggests it was a bit more like two nautical miles off the Cambodian coast and, in violation of maritime law, was not flying the flag of any nation. Khmer gunboats attacked the *Mayaguez*, boarded it, and seized control of the ship. Although never proven, most people believe that the *Mayaguez* was holding containers of equipment from the Saigon Embassy, which had been seized just days before. The president and the National Security Council met to discuss options, and perhaps because of the humiliation of the Saigon Embassy and the forced withdrawal of forces from Cambodia, there was a strong recommendation to act to end the seizure decisively. President Ford publicly called the seizure an act of piracy and acted accordingly with haste and force.

The navy dispatched the Knox-class frigate and sister ship of the

Robert E. Peckham, the USS *Harold E. Holt*, and the guided missile destroyer USS *Henry B. Wilson* and ordered marines based in Subic Bay and Okinawa to depart Subic Bay via aircraft to Thailand to prepare for an assault on the Khmer Rouge, while a 1,100-man battalion landing team assembled in Okinawa.

The Khmer troops extracted the crew of the *Mayaguez* and moved them to a small island named Koh Tang to be held as hostages. The USS *Holt* and over six hundred marines attempted to extract them. The hostages were then moved to the Cambodian mainland, while the USS *Holt* and a contingent of marines attacked Koh Tang. Three US helicopters were shot down, and fifteen marines were killed in the battle. Three marines were inadvertently left behind and were publicly executed by the Khmer Rouge. After the official end of the Vietnam conflict, marines and airmen were still dying. This, *officially*, however, was the last military incident, and these were the final military members *officially* killed during the Vietnam conflict. The Vietnam conflict era was declared over three days later on May 15, 1975, and the United States would never admit to any further casualties. Unfortunately, there were more to follow, which were never confirmed by the United States, and in truth, Squid Island was not the only island in which US troops were placed in harm's way.

In harm's way is an understatement. The North Vietnamese Army had been much like a bunch of Girl Scouts compared to the Khmer Rouge and the new Communist Party of Kampuchea (CPK). The Khmer Rouge regime was highly autocratic, xenophobic, paranoid, and beyond repressive. Huge numbers of deaths resulted from the regime's social engineering policies. Its attempts at agricultural reform through *social collectivization* directly led to ubiquitous famine. The CPV pathologically insisted on absolute self-sufficiency in everything, including the importation of medicine. This alone led to the deaths of many thousands from very treatable diseases, such as malaria. The Khmer Rouge regime murdered hundreds of thousands of people. Anyone viewed as a potential political opponent of its racist, xenophobic focus on the purity of the "traditional Cambodian" was executed. Anyone slightly connected with anyone who was a political opponent was murdered, and this led to the murder of any and every minority and dissident. Torture and completely arbitrary executions were implemented by its troops against anyone perceived as subversive. Estimates are that the Cambodian genocide led to the deaths of about two million people, which was at least a quarter of its population.

As Manny commanded his platoon, he was aware of much of the machinations involved in American politics in Indochina, and from his vantage point on Squid Island, he paid great attention to the briefings they received on a relatively sporadic basis. Manny lived with the possibility that things could heat up for this little group of Marines, but all indications were, at least for the moment, that they were relics and would soon be shipped home.

Daylight broke in the jungle, and Matt breathed a huge sigh of relief as the demons, imagined and real, became more manageable in his brain. With a great exhalation, Matt was reminded by a growl in his stomach that he had not eaten for two days. Even if he did not find food that day, his mission was much more important. He had to make it to his rendezvous point by the appointed time. As he warily slipped out of the tree that had been his bedroom the night before, he set out to check his snares on the off chance there might be food waiting. As he was doing so, his thoughts turned back to his early weeks on the *Robert E. Peckham*, and he smiled, remembering his friends, who seemed so very far away this day.

4

NICKNAMES AND WESTPACS

With some degree of effort, Wonder got out of his rack. "Racks" were essentially bunk beds, stacked three high in what was affectionately called by its residents, "the hole" and which the navy officially called a "berthing compartment." On the USS *Robert E. Peckham*, the operations/communications berthing compartment housed fifty-five sailors, spanned the width of the ship, and was perhaps thirty feet in length. This was the bedroom for all the radiomen, signalmen, operations specialists, sonarmen, navigators, hospital corpsmen, and the one lone postal clerk.

"Rack" was an appropriate term for the beds. To use the word *bunk* was somewhat of a stretch. The top bunk was a sheet metal platform, six feet long and two feet wide with two inches of foam rubber that served as a mattress. In about five hundred square feet resided every one of the sailors. Racks were assigned in accordance with seniority on the ship. The newest arrivals were assigned the top bunks, many of which were just inches from the overhead compartment lights and the tangle of wires ubiquitous to the entire ship. Those with more seniority got the bottom racks, the attraction being that they were in the dark. Those most senior got the middle racks. Hence, in the berthing compartment, it was easy to see who was most senior of the residents. There was no shortage of competition for the middle racks.

Matt marveled at the diversity of the personnel on his ship. Coming from a small town in New Mexico, he had little to no exposure to either minorities or ethnic diversity. He had never even met a black or Asian person. Yet here, all mixed up together, were not only African Americans but other extraordinary minorities that included Bostonians, Italians, Irish, Polish, Minnesotans, and Texans, among many other racial, social, and ethnic minorities.

As Matt was unpacking his belongings into his locker, he examined what was to be his bed. He was a tall and skinny guy, topping six and a half feet when he wasn't slouching. By his estimation, at most, the rack was six feet, which meant that he would need to find someplace to rest his spillover inches. He couldn't help but notice several other things. First, there was a large fluorescent overhead light that appeared to be no more than six inches from where his head would be when he slept. Next, there was the most amazing array of whirring noises coming from somewhere just below where he was standing. It was almost teeth-jarring, and he just couldn't imagine at that point how he was going to get two seconds of sleep down in this quasi-hell of a torture chamber.

As Matt was putting his stuff away from his sea bag into his tiny locker, Wonder began explaining things to him. "The *Bob E.* is an awesome ship, man," Wonder explained. "We've been on deployment six times in three years, which is a record for the nav. We've won three battle efficiency awards, or 'E's' as we call them. We are truly a steaming ship. And you have really good timing, as we are leaving on a Westpac cruise in three weeks."

Matt had heard about Westpacs in radioman school. From the sound of things, they were one long spree of drinking and fornication, which to a nineteen-year-old kid from Los Alamos, New Mexico, sounded very intriguing.

"But before I orient you anymore, you need to have a name, man," said Wonder. He stood up and fashioned a look akin to that of an aged Buddhist monk. "What did you say your civilian name was, kid?" asked Wonder.

"Matt Bertram," said Matt, feeling somewhat uncomfortable with the inspection he was receiving from this Texan Stevie Wonder.

"Ah," said Wonder, taking on a mystical look. "You look like that fucking nerd on Sesame Street. Pigman, what the fuck was his name?"

"Um, Big Bird?" said Pigman.

"No, not *that* fucking nerd," said Wonder. "The fucking nerd who collects paperclips," he specified.

"Bert?" Matt asked.

"Yeah, fucking Bert," agreed Wonder. "You are now and forevermore, 'Bert,'" pronounced Wonder.

Everyone in the compartment shouted, "Bert!" and apparently, it was a done thing. Matt would find that from that moment on in his life, nobody in his new naval realm would call him Matt. *Well, it could have been worse*, Matt (a.k.a., Bert) thought to himself. *At least I'm not Pigman.*

"Bert" would come to learn that Steve Wundar was from the small town of Rockdale, Texas, in the heart of watermelon country. He grew up on property that had originally been owned by his great-grandfather. His family was multigenerationally Southern Baptist, and Steve grew up in a household with no drinking, no gambling, no dancing, and no pretty much anything else that was fun. He was being groomed to be a pastor like his father and his granddaddy, right up until he and three of his friends were arrested for running stolen beer to one of the dry Texas counties and being involved in a multicounty police chase that resulted in Steve being given (only because the judge was also his uncle) the opportunity to enlist in the military or serve time in jail. The latter seemed especially uninteresting to Steve, so he enlisted in the navy. The day he raised his right hand to take the oath, he changed his handle to "Wonder," and a drunken, cussing, whoring Wonder took his rightful place as debaucher-in-chief of the *Robert E. Peckham*.

Wonder called the other guys in the compartment together and introduced them, one by one, to Bert. He called over a lanky guy with a deep Bostonian accent. "This is Skeeter," said Wonder. "He's got one of those unpronounceable Polish names, so he's Skeeter."

Behind Skeeter was an amazing guy with bright-red hair and a big bushy red beard. He looked as though he had just been rescued from a deserted island. "This is 'Shroom,'" said Wonder. "Shroom has a penchant for hallucinogenic drugs, mushrooms being his favorite. He doesn't make a lot of sense, but he'll grow on you."

Shroom proceeded to pull an old chicken leg bone out of his dungaree shirt pocket and hummed some marching song while pretending to play the chicken bone like a harmonica. At the end of his solo, everyone shouted something sounding like "*Bohicabec!*" Wonder explained that this was the *unofficial* motto of the USS *Robert E. Peckham* (known among the crew as the *Bob E. Chicken*) and stood for "Bend Over Here It Comes Again Bob E. Chicken." Out of the thousands of acronyms available in the navy, this was the most important acronym Bert would learn in his naval career.

Wonder proceeded to introduce the others, including "Red" another red-headed crew member, who would be Bert's leading petty officer in the radio shack, and "Happy," who literally looked happy all the time in a brain-damaged sort of way. Finally, Wonder explained that the chief petty officer of their division, SMC B. S. Boggs, lived in the chief's quarters when they were steaming someplace other than this and that their division officer, LTJG Hudson (whom they called "Rock" but not to his face) was in something called "Officer's Country," also apart from the enlisted berthing and strictly off limits to enlisted personnel, unless they were on official business. He was warned that Rock was an evil egotist who looked out for himself above all others. Rock had been an enlisted man and went to college and then to Officer Candidate School. "You might think a guy who served as enlisted would be fair-minded and friendly with other enlisted people," Wonder said, "but fuck that. He hates enlisted men and thinks he is God's great gift to the *Bob E.* Don't, *don't* get on his bad side, or your life will be living hell," was his unambiguous warning.

"You are in luck to be on the good ole *Bob E.*," said Wonder. "Our CO, Commander Stilton, is a son of a bitch, but he's divorced so he lives on the ship and is ex-merchant marine. Those two things mean that the *Bob E.* is steaming practically all the time!"

"Sorry, Wonder, but what exactly is steaming?" Matt inquired.

"Steaming? Steaming?" said Wonder. With a look of absolute incredulity, Wonder explained it this way: "Fucking steaming is when we are underway, headed for someplace else. Steaming is what we sailors on the *Bob E.* fucking live for! And when we get underway in two weeks, you'll see for yourself that when you start steaming, you leave the real world and enter a new reality, kind of like the Twilight Zone, only drunk off your ass. The *Bob E.* becomes our huge, ugly, gray, slow magic carpet, and when she's steaming, it means you're about to go someplace fucking fantastic. It could be Subic Bay, it could be Kao Shung, Mombassa, or it could be Bangkok. It will lead you to adventures you won't be able to describe, especially to your dear old mother. But wherever you go, your balls will grow fur, and your liver will scream. Oh, and odds are, you'll need a penicillin shot afterward. But first, we need to take you up to the chief's quarters and introduce you to Chief Boggs."

Bert was to learn later that the penicillin shot was no exaggeration from Wonder's standpoint. He regularly bragged that he had a punch card at sick bay for his shots. Although it was never proven, many of Bert's fellow crewmembers claimed that Wonder had gonorrhea five times and syphilis twice just during the last Westpac cruise. That seemed to Bert to be cause for some degree of alarm, but it was apparently a badge of honor among Wonder's brethren.

5

B.S

B.S. Boggs was the chief petty officer in charge of the "OC" division on the *Bob E.* OC stood for "operations-communications" and included radiomen, who were in the belly of the ship communicating by radio, and signalmen, who stood on the flying deck of the ship and communicated by semaphore, flags, and flashing lights. In this time long before email and the Internet, these two groups were the lifeline to the world, especially when they were hundreds of miles from a naval base. The most senior chief, whether a radioman or signalman, was the enlisted person in charge of the division and reported directly to the communications officer. On a small ship like the *Bob E.*, the communication officer was usually a brand-new ensign or LT JG, and if the Com-O was smart, he relied heavily upon the experience and credibility of the chief petty officer in charge.

As they walked into the chief's mess, it was obviously a different place—a bit nicer (but not that much) than the regular crew quarters, with a table in the middle of one room for meals and a much smaller berthing compartment than the hole. Just as off-limits as "officer country" (where the officers berthed), the chiefs' quarters were entered by nonchiefs only with permission or on an important mission. Chief Boggs was always okay with the introduction of new meat.

Wonder knocked on the outer door, and with a "What the fuck do you want?" (which apparently was permission to enter), the two walked in. At the table were two chiefs playing cribbage, apparently for money. "Chief, this is the new guy in the radio shack, and I wanted to introduce you," said Wonder.

Signalman Chief Petty Officer B. S. Boggs was, to many, a most interesting man. To Matt, now Bert, Chief Boggs looked a bit like a skid-row drunk who hadn't shaved or showered for several weeks, wearing a very wrinkled khaki uniform and the gold anchors of a chief on his collar. When he spoke, Chief Boggs was practically unintelligible, due mostly to the fact that he had no teeth. B.S. did have dentures, but the man loathed them and felt like he was gagging whenever they were in his mouth. Consequently, he wore them only when he had to wear them, which was mostly when he was at home with his wife, Adelle, because she forced him to wear them. B.S. had "lost" seven sets of dentures in the past—"lost" meaning that when he was drunk (which was quite often), he would tear them out of his mouth at some point and rid himself of the maddening fake choppers. The navy had told him that this was the last set they were paying for, so now Adelle guarded the teeth with her life.

Chief Boggs had been in the navy for twenty-six years and had very far from a sterling record. It was rumored he had gained rank from E-1 (seaman recruit) to E-6 (first class petty officer) three times, having had been busted back to E-1 each of those times. Although Chief Boggs never discussed it, Wonder told Matt that B.S. had been assigned to a PBR in Vietnam. The PBR was the navy's designation for a small rigid-hulled patrol boat used in Vietnam. These fast-attack riverboats were deployed in a force that grew to over 250 boats, the most common craft in the River Patrol Force, and were used to stop and search river traffic in areas such as the Rung Sat Special Zone, the Mekong Delta, and the Saigon River, among others. The boats filled a vital mission to protect ground troops and to attempt to disrupt weapons shipments. In this role, these small boats very often were involved in firefights with enemy soldiers on boats and on the shore, were used to insert and extract Navy SEAL teams, and went on other missions. The majority of sailors who were killed in action in Vietnam crewed these boats. Wonder explained that the chief had been a first-class petty officer on a boat commanded by a brand-new ensign three weeks out of the naval academy. When the boat drew fire from NVA troops, the ensign froze, and Chief Boggs abruptly made sure the ensign was out of gunfire by hitting him with the butt of an M-16, took control of the boat, and saved the crew from serious peril. He was brought up on charges of assaulting his commanding officer, was busted to E-1, and was awarded the Bronze Star for valor, all on the same day.

As Bert stood in the chief's mess waiting for some recognition of his presence, the chief looked up, closed one eye, and said something completely unintelligible that sounded a lot like "inagaddadavita," which Bert completely missed. An excruciatingly long silence passed, and the chief said, this time, a bit more understandably, "Hey, you fucking asshole, can't you see I'm busy? See you at muster tomorrow." Bert had no idea what that meant, but he and Wonder left without further word.

6

FIRST MUSTER AND THE ROCK

The next morning at 0700, the ship began its workday with what was known as "muster." Essentially, every division on the ship had a particular place that they would meet each morning for roll call and a traditional military welcome to the day. Bert was still completely lost on the ship, so he was careful to follow the other radiomen and signalmen to the top of the signal bridge, where operations-communications, or OC division, mustered. Traditionally, the division officer and the senior enlisted man administered the muster. Still waiting for their division officer, LTJG Hudson, to arrive, Chief Boggs called the roll, conducted a very cursory uniform inspection, and told dirty jokes, none of which was understandable to Bert. Bert thought to himself, *I've got to learn how to understand this guy, or I'm in trouble.*

As if on cue, LTJG Hudson (a.k.a. Rock) swaggered in with timing obviously designed to place all the focus on himself. Grabbing the clipboard from Chief Boggs, Hudson started with what Bert would soon learn was his standard soliloquy. "I've got a few announcements to make. As you are aware, because of my quick learning, I'll soon be moving on to being ship's navigator. You probably don't know this, but this is an important position on the ship, and as such, none of you are going to fuck this up for me. You will stay sharp, your uniforms will be squared-away, and we will be volunteering for a few extra details during the coming weeks so that the XO will be confident that this division has been run as a well-oiled machine. Speaking of which, I have no doubt that someone snuck into Officer's Country last week and replaced my hair oil with actual oil. You all are suspect, and when I find the miscreants who did this, they will have my wrath, which none of you wants, I promise." The announcement seemed a bit out of place for the setting, but Bert would come to know that the words, "You will have my wrath, I promise," were the most common words that escaped out of Hudson's mouth.

"Now," Rock continued without skipping a beat, "I understand that we have a new member of our division, RMSN Bertram. Please welcome RMSN Bertram to our division and make him feel at home. And because I'm up for the promotion, I want *no* hazing of Bertram until I move to navigation, or you will have my wrath, I promise. Bertram, we will meet in the radio shack for a briefing in ten minutes. That is all." With a wave of what Bert thought was probably an invisible swagger stick, as quickly as LTJG Hudson arrived, he also vanished.

Following muster, one of the crew members who was not present the previous night came up to introduce himself. An incredibly handsome young man with a shock of black hair and a winsome smile stuck out his hand. "Bert, right?" the young man said. "They call me Lucky. Good to meet you!"

As Bert shook Lucky's hand, Lucky rolled his eyes and said, "I know, first question is, how did Wonder come up with that one, right?"

Bert shook his head as he was shaking Lucky's hand.

"Well, Bert, my real name is Patrick O'Malley. Yeah, you guessed it, I'm *Italian*," he said, with a wink. In a thick Bostonian accent, Lucky explained in a way that sounded to Bert like, "Da only Irish guy Wondah knew was the leprechahn on the Lucky Chahms box.

So, blam, dat's me." Bert had never heard a Bostonian accent from anyone outside of television. Although not as difficult to understand as Chief Boggs's speech, Lucky's accent still required some interpretation. It seemed to Bert that people from Boston replaced all of the final "r's" in a word with "h." Bert thought it was endearing and enjoyed hearing Lucky talk, which Lucky did, almost incessantly. It turned out that Lucky had only been on the ship a few weeks longer than Bert but had served two years on another ship as a signalman. Lucky had a reputation as a guy who could find things not readily available elsewhere for you. Lucky was constantly immersed in, if not black-market commerce, at least *gray*-market commerce. Lucky had everything and anything that ran in short supply on the ship, and Bert soon learned that he could get a Snickers "bah" and a Coke twenty-four hours a day from Lucky for a slight duty above retail.

"So, I hear you went to teletype repair school, huh, Bert?" said Lucky. When Bert affirmed that, Lucky looked side to side and said as though the CIA were listening, "Let me know if you need me to get any 'pahts' for you for your teletypes. I got some amazing connections."

Bert thanked Lucky and let him know that he had to go to meet LTJG Hudson and probably didn't want to be late for that meeting.

While Bert had gained some expertise in finding his way about the ship, he went down two wrong passageways and one wrong ladder before finding his way to his destination.

"You are one minute late, Seaman Bertram," LTJG Hudson snarled. "You're new here, so I'll give you grace this one time. Do it again, and you will have my wrath. I promise."

"Aye aye, sir," Bert squeaked out. Having never really had much opportunity to associate with officers, Bert was overly intimidated by the khaki uniforms and shiny bars on officers' collars.

"I do want to welcome you to the ship, son," said Hudson more cordially. Bert thought that using the word *son* to a person who was probably six or seven years younger was a bit odd but unworthy of comment. "We have been in need of a teletype repairman for a couple of months now, and we've had to limp into port on several occasions and have repairmen from the USS *Ashtabula* come over to fill in when we're in port. That's hell on my division budget, and with my promotion coming up, I need to make my budget look good, so I'm counting on you to keep the teletypes in good shape." Teletypes were a critical part of a radio shack and were the primary method of communications both between ships and from ships to naval communication stations. Even a small radio shack like the *Peckham* had three UGC-6 teletype machines with paper tape transmission and a bank of UGC-25 receive-only teletypes. Inside the machine was a very sophisticated printer that had six clutches, over six hundred springs, and such an abundance of adjustments it was impossible to count and virtually impossible to keep them running well for long. If one clutch, spring, or adjustment went out of configuration, the printer would print garbled distortions of messages, creating the possibility of missing messages or critical instructions. The teletype technology currently used on the *Bob E.* was developed in the 1950s, and there had not been much of an update since then. The teletypes were constantly breaking, and, consequently, having onboard repair personnel was critical to smooth and accurate communications.

"You need to know that we are short-handed in the shack, and so you'll be standing regular radio watches in addition to repairing the teletypes. When things are slow in the shack, I expect you at the workbench maintaining and making repairs. Don't let me down. This is important for my upcoming promotion, and I'll have my eyes on you like a lion on an antelope. Understand?"

"Yes, Mr. Hudson, I understand, sir," Bert once again barely squeaked out.

When Bert had the opportunity to give the teletypes close inspection, it became clear they were a mess. Out of five of the receive-only printers, only three were working, and one of the big UGC-6s wasn't functional. Bert had his work cut out for him.

When the ship was in a port with a naval communications station, the *Peckham* could shift all the teletype communications to the station, and one radioman on duty could drive to the station to pick up the ship's messages on a regular basis. The communications stations were few and far between, however, so when they were at Pearl Harbor or Subic Bay, duty was much easier than when they were practically anyplace else.

Because there were fewer radioman duties to occupy his time in port, Bert had the opportunity to work on teletypes. This, of course, didn't relieve him of the other tasks that someone with low rank had to do, including swabbing and buffing the decks, cleaning the heads, doing preventive maintenance on the antennas, and being rounded up to a work party any time supplies were delivered to the ship.

Of all the jobs Bert was assigned, using the electric floor buffer was the most frightening for him. Bert had had a truly bad experience while he was in San Diego at the naval training center. There were a couple of weeks between graduating from boot camp and starting radioman school, and he was placed in a pool of base labor during that time. His first day on the job, he was assigned to assist in cleaning the base commander's offices. Bert had never even seen an electric floor polisher but was given the duty to buff the floor in the hallway outside of the CO's office. Along the hallway was a trophy case with glass doors containing an array of trophies and awards the base and the CO had received. With no instruction on how to use the buffer, Bert proceeded to grab the handlebars and squeeze a lever to start the floor buffer. The buffer bucked and swung left and right, completely out of Bert's control. The buffer swung wildly into the trophy case, knocking it over, breaking the windows, and damaging a number of the CO's prized trophies. For the rest of his tenure in the labor force, Bert emptied garbage from the mess hall and cleaned the noxious-smelling loading dock and dumpsters. The fear of floor buffers rose to the level of terror. As such, Bert was willing to trade that duty for absolutely any other duty, no matter how unpleasant.

Bert's first experience with a new term, *work party*, came on his second day on the ship, when Chief Boggs rounded up some of his men to bring boxes of supplies and food on the ship. Wonder was among those recruited, and so he grabbed Bert as they were heading to the work party. "Come with me, Bert. I'm going to show you a classic navy skill called 'skating,'" said Wonder.

As they headed down to the pier, Wonder and Bert both grabbed boxes, but Wonder said to the petty officer directing the party, "These are headed to the wardroom. We'll take them there." They headed onboard the ship, each with a box, and went up to the signal bridge rather than heading to Officer's Country. Wonder opened a door, and they stepped into the emergency radio shack, a seldom-used room that served as a backup to the radio shack in the event it was disabled during an attack or emergency. Wonder sat down in one of the two chairs and said, "We've got at least a half an hour before the work party is over. Time for us to take a little 'nooner,'" and with that, Wonder leaned back, shut his eyes, and within seconds was snoring. Bert assumed the word *nooner* was the navy term for nap, so, taking Wonder's lead, he did the same himself.

Bert was just drifting off to a quiet nap when the door to the room opened, and there, red-faced and looking like Jack the Ripper, stood LTJG Hudson. "What in the *fuck* do you think you are doing?" Hudson gurgled. "Get your lazy asses back to the pier. I'm right behind you." In a march of shame, the two moved quickly back to the work party, and once they arrived, Rock yelled to the entire work party crew, "These two lazy sailors decided *you* should work harder than they and were hard at work *skating* when you were hard at work doing your job. I want all of you to stop working, have a seat here, and you can watch SM3 Wundar and RMSN Bertram do your work for you." Turning to the two troublemakers, he said in a very low, shaking, and almost uncontrolled tone, "You are now going to find out what my wrath looks like. Your reprobate asses are mine. When you are done here, I'm going to find more fun for you until you learn that I am in charge and you never, never cross me. I explained that I'm up for a promotion to navigator, and if you so much as put one bump in that for me from now on, you will have my wrath, I promise. Bertram, this is your second day on the *Peckham*. This is going to be a long, miserable ride for you if you don't get your ass squared-away."

Wonder and Bert spent the next three hours carrying boxes while the others looked on, obviously enjoying the break. For the next month, anytime there was a crappy job to be done, Rock assigned it to Bert. If extra duty was needed, Bert got it. Fortunately, as Rock, Bert, and Wonder hoped, Rock soon was awarded his navigator job, which meant a new division officer for OC division, so on a day-to-day basis, their paths rarely crossed. On a small ship, however, it's tough to stay out of sight forever.

7

SOUND-POWERED PHONE BATTERIES, BT PUNCHES, AND OTHER FORMS OF TORTURE

By the end of the third day on the *Bob E.*, Bert, by no small bit of effort and trial and error, had figured out how to travel to the mess deck for meals, the *hole* to sleep, and the radio shack for work. Bert marveled at the array of alternate terms for common things on a ship. The bathroom was a "head," the walls were "bulkheads," the ceiling was the "overhead," the floor was the "deck," the doors were "hatches," and the toilets were "shitters" among many, many other things. Even people had terms. Anyone who did anything electronic, including radiomen, were *Twidgets*. Anyone in engineering was a *Snipe*. Most senior enlisted called officers (not to their faces, of course) *Zeroes*. Signalmen were *Skivvy Wavers* and so on. Due to the plethora of alternate terms, the primary form of entertainment for Bert's new shipmates was apparently taking advantage of this fact in a very unpleasant hazing ritual for new sailors. Bert spent the better part of a day completing a requisition for "sound-powered phone batteries" and being sent all over the ship to various authorities only to find out that sound-powered phones were named that for a reason. Matt was told to find a quart of iD1oT and spent the better part of the day searching for this mythical substance. It wasn't until the end of the workday that Matt was told it was pronounced as "one dee ten tee," "one delta ten tango," or "idiot." The hazing continued when Matt was sent to engineering to get a "BT punch." BT stood for boiler technician. The BTs were widely held by Twidgets to be the most badass sailors on the ship. Bert did succeed in getting a BT punch right in the eye, which gave him a big shiner, a billboard advertisement to everyone he encountered for the next several days that he was new onboard.

When Bert wasn't being hazed, he was doing all the jobs that the least senior person in the division does, including scrubbing the *shitters*, swabbing the floors (an alternative term for mopping), and general crap work. Bert had learned the day prior that "work parties" were no parties at all but were a regular part of the day in the life of a junior sailor. The extra shit work that Rock gave Bert in unending portions added to the burden. In addition to the ancillary work, Bert was being taught his job as a radioman. Although Bert had gone to radioman school for three months, he found that what he learned in school had relatively little application in the fleet. Just one instance became clear in Bert's mind. One day, Red, the leading petty officer of the radio shack, brought him into the transmitter room to fire up their HF transmitter. Bert had remembered the instructor when he was at "A" school, carefully explaining that this transmitter was incredibly expensive, sensitive, and needed to be treated with the utmost care and that it had to be turned on for use in a very specific way and treated like a Tiffany lamp because of its delicate and highly expensive nature. Red showed him where the transmitter was and told Bert to set it up. Bert began the methodical process of setting it up, and when he was done, nothing happened. He tried one more time to no avail. Red laughed and said, "Where in the fuck did you learn that, kid? Step aside, and I'll show you the right way." Red stepped back and gave the transmitter a Bruce Lee–style roundhouse kick right in the side, and the transmitter came buzzing to life.

"I can see you got a lot to learn," said Red, as he walked out the door. So much for sensitive equipment.

One other bit of language that Bert was still getting used to was the distinctive way people spoke English in the navy. Apparently, it was critical to use the word *fuck* at least once, maybe twice, in every single sentence. The speaker also apparently received extra credit for inserting that profanity in the middle of a multisyllabic word, such as "I want you to be at the purser's office at one-fucking-thirty this afternoon" or "squared afuckingway." Bert was a bit reluctant to start using this word in any consistent fashion, still remembering the soap taste in his mouth for swearing when he was growing up. After a bit of practice, however, he was amazed at how quickly he became accustomed to this new language, which he discovered was not just a profanity but also an adverb, adjective, verb, and noun, depending upon the context. It was un*fucking*real and as it turned out, a very cathartic way to communicate.

As Bert walked out of the transmitter room, he was greeted by an officer. "Bert," said Red, "I want to introduce you to the officer who is going to take LTJG Hudson's place as division officer, Ensign Crosby."

"Good morning, sir," said Bert. "It is very nice to meet you." Bert quickly made a mental bet that Wonder would be calling him *Bing* soon.

Ensign Crosby looked Bert up and down and said, "Nice to meet you, kid. Just do whatever these fine sailors tell you to do, and you'll do okay. I'm a graduate of the US Naval Academy, kid, which really doesn't mean shit, other than, if I want a good career as a navy officer, I'll be kissing khaki asses all over this ship, and I won't have any time for you. I don't understand a damn thing in this radio shack, and I don't want to. So, don't ever ask me any questions that make me look stupid in front of the other officers, and we'll get along just fine."

With that, Ensign Crosby walked out. Red walked over and said, "Glad you had a chance to meet Bing. Get it, *Bing* Crosby! But don't ever call him that to his face. It's Wonder's name for him, but the officers don't get to know what we call them. He's a good guy, but he's right. He's completely oblivious and dumber than dirt. I guess that's what it takes to be Zero in the navy today."

Bert gave himself a mental high five for getting that nickname right.

Things on the *Bob E.* were very busy, as the crew was preparing to leave for a Western Pacific deployment, commonly termed a "West-pac." While maintenance was the top of the list, the guys in the radio shack began regaling Bert with stories of their adventures and what he could anticipate. "Subic Bay is like a huge circus," Wonder told Bert. Bert had heard about Westpacs since radioman school but never from anyone who had experienced them in person.

On the third day of Bert's tenure on the *Bob E.*, the guys took him to the enlisted men's club for beers and to listen to some good country music. Bert had always been a hard rock kind of guy, Led Zeppelin, Aerosmith, AC/DC, Deep Purple, and Black Sabbath being his favorites. As they walked into the club, a decidedly different kind of music was being played. The navy enlisted service was very good at bringing mainland bands to Hawaii to entertain the troops. While Bert had never been to one of the famed USO shows, coming from New Mexico, he thought the entertainment at the enlisted clubs was great. He heard strange music from bands like Charlie Daniels, Hank Williams, Marshall Tucker, Willie Nelson, and Waylon Jennings, among others, only in the guise of the Yellow Rose Band, brought straight from Texas. Wonder explained as each song played. Bert only listened casually, as he had always regarded country music as annoying and stupid. Apparently, this was now the music of choice among his new shipmates.

As the band played their rendition of Conway Twitty's "Hello, Darlin,'" Wonder, with a hush all around him, leaned over, smiled, and said, "Imagine getting anything you want, and I mean *anything* you want, for less than ten bucks. That is Subic Bay, dude!" Obviously, Texas was far from everyone's thoughts. The thoughts were more toward the upcoming deployment.

"Anything," said Shroom, "including women, drugs, and even having someone killed."

The guys explained that Subic Bay Naval Base in the Philippines was to be their primary destination on the cruise and would serve as the base that they sailed out of in the South China Sea for the next six months. Olongapo was the city just outside of Naval Base Subic Bay and was an entirely different land. "When we get there, you'll exchange your US money for pesos, but we call 'em 'circus tickets,' and you'll understand what we mean by that when we get there," said Pigman.

"The food," said Shroom, "is to die for—lumpia, pandesal, adobo, pancit, and others. But the one thing *nobody* will eat is balut."

"Balut, huh?" said Bert. "What the *fuck* is that?" He was already getting fond of the "F" word, and as he really wanted to fit in with these guys, he was actively overusing it.

"Balut is just disgusting, and even the weirdest, most abnormal people on earth avoid it," said Wonder. "They take a duck egg that's fertilized, let the embryo half-grow, then they cook it halfway, and bury it in the ground for three months. There are vendors who sell it from carts early in the morning. You can't even get within ten feet of a balut that's been cracked. But it's not only the smell. It's eating that little baby bird with the crunchy beak and feet and bones and the half-cooked slime. Nobody can hold it down."

"I'll bet I can eat a balut when we get there," Bert said. He wasn't certain that he had said that out loud and immediately regretted it, but he was really trying to be one of the guys.

"No possible fucking way," said Shroom. "Nobody will eat that shit."

"Well, Bert," said Wonder, "you are an amazingly stupid person. I'll just chock it up to ignorance, but ... I'll take that bet. Let's just bet an anything you want at Marilyn's Number One that you won't be able to eat it and keep it down."

"What is that?" said Bert.

"Anything means *anything*, dumbass," said Wonder. "There are these amazing massage parlors that offer any delight known to man. If you eat it and keep it down, I'll buy one for you, and if you can't, it's a super-deluxe-everything-included fucking massage for me at Marilyn's in Olongapo on your dime."

The consensus was that out of all the massage parlors/whorehouses in Olongapo, Marilyn's #1 was the very best. It had the biggest "menu" in town, cheap prices, and the lowest rate of venereal disease in the city. Marilyn's advertised heavily by having children pass out discounted "massage" cards to sailors as they crossed the bridge from Naval Base Subic Bay into town, and it seemed to be effective. Everyone knew of Marilyn's. Everyone.

So, the bet was on. Not only had Bert never eaten anything more exotic than his mother's pot roast, he had certainly never eaten anything close to balut and had absolutely never had a super-deluxe-everything-included massage. He was already regretting taking this bet.

8

UNDERWAY

The weeks prior to a ship's deployment were very busy ones. During deployment, US Navy ships spend many weeks, often alone or in small groups, in the vast, empty ocean. Consequently, it is the crew's job to be certain everything possible is in good working order and the ship is well-supplied and ready for the many perils that the ocean presents. This includes short periods underway in order to test engines, radios, and the myriad of other equipment onboard. Coming and going on these short trials gave Bert the opportunity to see Pearl Harbor from a unique vantage point. Naval Base Pearl Harbor was a beautiful place, with tall palm trees and warm air. Bert was amazed to see that several of the battleships sunk during the Pearl Harbor attack remained in place, underwater. He was aware of the USS *Arizona* memorial, but just walking to the end of the peer, he could see in the harbor, not fifteen feet from where he was walking, were the remains of several other ships, only ten or twenty feet into the harbor from the peer. The sight gave Bert an immediate sense of the history of war and the grave consequences of the attack on Pearl Harbor.

The first day that Bert was a part of the *Peckham* getting underway was incredibly exciting. If only a two-day sea trial, Red told Bert that he could go topside to watch the *Bob E.* depart the pier and the harbor. Because the signalmen were part of Bert's division, they let him come up on the signal bridge where they stood watch. Using semaphore flags and flashing lights, the signalmen communicated with other ships and the harbor master. As people on the pier dropped the massive lines holding the *Bob E.* to the pier, the ship gave three blasts on its immense horn to indicate they were underway. Tugs brought the ship to the middle of the harbor at which point the captain took over and guided the USS *Robert E. Peckham* past Ford Island, where the airfield that was attacked by the Japanese was located, to the entrance of the harbor. Looking down, Bert saw thousands of jellyfish floating beside them, and then just as they were leaving the harbor for open ocean, suddenly, out of nowhere, a group of dolphins began swimming in the bow wake of the ship as if to escort the gray behemoth out to sea. The languorous Hawaiian air felt like a gentle massage on Bert's face. Just outside the harbor, the water turned a spectacular emerald blue and then gradually became darker as the ocean's bottom sank to thousands of feet in depth. It was exhilarating, and after that first breathtaking time, Bert never missed the experience. In many future times underway, Bert would feel the adrenaline pump through his veins each time those three horn blasts sounded. Over the few weeks prior to leaving for deployment, Bert would experience this feeling often, as the *Bob E.* tested engines and weapons systems at sea in preparation for the day they would head overseas.

The USS *Robert E. Peckham* was one of forty-six Knox-class frigates that the navy commissioned between 1969 and 1974. The ships were designed in the early 1950s, and the first of its class, the USS *Knox*, was commissioned in 1969. The Knox-class ships were about 438 feet long overall. They were the last of the ships built with a steam-plant propulsion system and a single screw, making them slow and difficult to sail. With 216 officers and crew, the ship was small by US Navy standards, which was a bonus from a cruise perspective, as it meant the ship could dock at many ports the larger navy ships could not.

These ships were designed primarily for two purposes. First, they were equipped for antisubmarine warfare and had an amazing array of sonar equipment, including an amazing little sonar fish that could be dropped on a tethered line behind the ship. Second, they were designed to escort aircraft carriers on their missions. Their primary job was, in the face of attack, to have the enemy shoot at them instead of the carrier. They carried electronic equipment to make them look bigger on radar than they actually were and had a bubble machine on the hull to make them sound on sonar like much larger ships. "Decoy" was the word Wonder used to describe the *Bob E.*'s mission. "We're just a lure for the enemy, and our life expectancy under attack is just under thirty seconds." Bert realized he could have gotten a better ship assignment when he heard that.

Wonder's theory was bolstered by the fact that the ship had very little in the way of weapons. The *Bob E.* had a five-inch gun forward, an eight-round ASROC launcher (with sixteen missiles carried) abaft the gun and forward of the bridge, and four fixed antisubmarine torpedo tubes. A small helicopter deck and hangar for operating a small antisubmarine helicopter called a LAMPS was fitted aft. In addition, the *Bob E.* had a little more armament than the earlier Knox-class frigates. On the aft deck, the ship was fitted with an eight-round basic point-to-point defense missile system (BPDMS) launcher for Sea Sparrow missiles. To Bert, that sounded like a lot of good stuff, but his shipmates who had served on destroyers and cruisers laughed at what they called the "rubber-band guns" that the *Bob E.* had. By the time the *Bob E.* was commissioned in 1972, the ships were already on the drawing board for decommissioning and were known in the Pentagon and among a future generation of destroyermen as "McNamara's Folly." Nevertheless, the *Bob E. Chicken* was now Bert's home, and he hoped he would never have to find out what the actual life expectancy was under attack.

The night before deployment, B.S. held an official, "if you don't come, you'll do extra duty pre-deployment" party in his small base housing apartment. Adelle had made some wonderful comfort food, which the sailors would not see for the next six months, and the entire communications division was there. This was the first time that Bert had had a chance to see the chief in civilian attire. All protocols regarding rank and status were left behind. Bert marveled at B.S.'s capacity for alcohol. He had never seen one man chug a quart of vodka, only to tell a joke without taking a breath. At one point in the evening, B.S. called Bert, Wonder, and Shroom into the tiny living room, pulled out yet another bottle of vodka, unscrewed the lid, and promptly guzzled approximately half of the bottle. He then placed the cap in his mouth with flourish, much like a magician about to perform an amazing trick and did a backflip onto his backside in the middle of the living room floor. Bert stood in amazement as the chief shook his head and then looked up and proudly produced the bottle cap from his mouth, obviously expecting applause, which the three amply provided. Although the chief invited Bert to repeat the trick, he was saved by Adelle entering the room with a reproving look as she grabbed Bert. She pushed Bert out of the room, shouting over her shoulder, "I'm going to kidnap Bert for just a second, B.S. You boys keep playing."

Adelle placed a wrestler-worthy lock on Bert's arm and walked him into the kitchen. "I have a very important mission for you, Bert," said Adelle. "It's not optional, and I won't let you say no."

The gravity of the look on Adelle's face forced Bert to nod his head and say, "Anything, Adelle. Just name it."

"Well, Bert, you know that B.S. hates those dentures of his, correct?" said Adelle.

"Yeah, I've heard that, but I wish he'd wear them more. I have real trouble understanding him when he doesn't."

"I know, Bert. You'll get used to it. Everyone does eventually. But here's the thing. He's on his seventh set in three years, and the navy has told him they won't pay for any more lost dentures, and on our salary, we can't afford to buy him new ones. B.S. has *never* returned from a deployment with his dentures. Never. He drinks too much, gets pissed, and tosses them away."

"I've heard," said Bert. "What can I do to help?"

"Quite simply, I want you to guard B.S.'s dentures as though you were a Secret Service agent guarding the president. He *must* come back with those dentures." Adelle's eyes met Bert's, and Bert had a sudden feeling that this just might be more responsibility than he was capable of managing.

"You've got it, Adelle," Bert said with a look of intense seriousness on his face. "He will come back with those dentures. I promise." Little did Bert know, but this seemingly small promise would change his life forever.

9

WESTPAC

Finally, early the next morning, with a mass crew hangover, a navy tradition began expressing itself as the *Robert E. Peckham* left for its Westpac deployment. Each officer and crew member, attired in dress whites, stood at parade rest, lining the rails of the USS *Robert E. Peckham.* As lines were cast off, the now familiar three blasts of the ship's horn proclaimed the start of Bert's much-anticipated adventure. Families lined the pier, waving goodbye to their loved ones with air-kisses and tears as the tugboats escorted the vessel out into the harbor. It was also tradition to sail by the offices of the harbor master and the office of the commanding admiral of the Third Fleet, which were both on Ford Island. The *Peckham* flew flags of Destroyer Squadron Twenty-Three, the Third Fleet, and, of course, the United States of America. The entire impressive scene brought goose bumps to Bert as he stood at the rails of the *Bob E.* It was a truly magnificent experience for him as well as the other sailors lining the rails.

The *Bob E.* would be gone for six months, with an itinerary of Subic Bay; Yokosuka, Japan; Bangkok, Thailand; Pusan, Korea; Singapore, Malaysia; and various other stops. Patrol missions were set for the Indian Ocean, the South China Sea, and the Gulf of Thailand. It would be a busy time, with plenty of work to be done at sea. The radio shack was manned twenty-four hours each day and was always buzzing with the sound of radio communication, cryptographic machines, and teletypes. The command officers of the navy communicated with the fleet through something called the "fleet broadcast," which was sent via HF receivers, passed through cryptographic machines that were reset with a specific code each day, and then on to teletype machines. The radiomen would watch the broadcast and separate messages into general for everyone and those specific to the *Bob E.* and would deliver those messages to the appropriate departments on the ship, either by carrying them or sending them through "bunny tubes," which were vacuum-controlled tubes going to the bridge and combat information centers on the ship, much like the vacuum tubes in department stores and banks. Depending upon where they were in the world, the high-frequency broadcasts could be easy or more difficult to receive. The fleet broadcast was on over twenty frequencies, and much of the radiomen's job was to keep the receivers dialed to a clear frequency. The radiomen very often spent an entire watch with headphones on, manually dialing and redialing the receivers to find the best frequencies and then resynching the crypto equipment so the messages could be received. In addition, the radiomen would communicate with other ships in their squadron, both via ship-to-ship teletypes and voice. When not much else was going on, very often, the radiomen would chat with amateur HAM radio operators around the world, who were always thrilled to talk to a US Navy ship.

Lucky had become Bert's closest friend on the ship, and even though they did different jobs, Bert would spend a good deal of time on the signal bridge, which was a lookout bridge above the actual bridge of the ship. It was where the signalmen flashed lights, did semaphore, and hung various pennants that spelled out messages to others at sea. Bert was never bored when he was with Lucky, first because Lucky talked incessantly and second because Lucky's watches were regularly interrupted with people coming by to barter for snacks, beer, cigarettes, and a variety of interesting men's entertainment magazines.

Watches at sea were typically "port and starboard," which meant the radiomen stood watches of eight hours on and eight hours off. Bert would start with an 8:00 a.m. to 4:00 p.m. day shift, be off from 4:00 p.m. until midnight, and then back on from midnight until 8:00 a.m. As the watches were never the same on successive days, it made for difficult and irregular sleep, which made it difficult to keep one's focus on tasks at hand. Additionally, when the fleet broadcast frequencies were difficult to find, it unnerved the cryptographic machines, which caused an endless and unraveling repetition of *beep beep beeps*. Very often, after a difficult watch, Bert would good to bed only to continue to hear the beeps in his restless sleep. Nevertheless, the good part of port and starboard watches was that it allowed for sailors at sea to catch a movie every other evening and still have some semblance of a day job occasionally on that same rotation schedule.

Due to Bert's additional duties repairing the persistently malfunctioning teletypes, there was little time for recreation when not on watch. Bert was always under pressure, as once a teletype printer broke, the entire teletype was out of commission until the printer was repaired. The printer could easily be removed from the teletype and repaired at the bench, but Bert always had at least one printer in the process of repair. The frustration was only intensified with Hudson's constant haranguing over having all of the teletypes up and running.

One evening, when Bert was hanging out on the signal bridge with Lucky, he shared his frustration over the printers with him. Lucky, listening intently, patiently waited for Bert to finish and said, "I don't know anything about these teletypes, Bert, but it seems to me that if you had an extra printer that was working, it'd take the pressure off just to pop out the broken one, pop in the working one, and then work on the broken printer at your leisure, right?"

"Of course it would, but these printers are like six thousand dollars each, and they would never give me the budget to buy one, even if it made complete sense," Bert ruminated.

"I'll just bet," said Lucky, "that I can work a deal to get one. I'll bet it would be easier than finding the extra binoculars I got for our signalmen or the color TV I got for the officers in the wardroom."

Bert let Lucky know that would be fantastic, doubting that even Lucky, the dealmaker of the century, could pull that one off and not giving it much thought once he headed back to the radio shack.

When the *Bob E.* would be in port, most of the crew no longer was needed on a shift basis, and so most of the sailors had the opportunity to work on the ship doing maintenance, painting, or cleaning during the day and play at night. Unfortunately for the radiomen, their job continued as usual when in port, so they had to manage continuing their shifts on port and starboard watches while at the same time having as much liberty ashore as possible. This often resulted in either inebriation or hangover while on watch, as well as a constant state of sleep deprivation.

Naval Base Subic Bay was the largest naval base in the Western Pacific. The base had a long history, going back to the 1700s when the Philippines was a Spanish colony. The base was over 262 square miles in size and boasted the largest navy exchange in the world. The Vietnam War turned Subic Bay into the US Seventh Fleet's forward base for repair and replenishment after the Gulf of Tonkin incident in 1964. By 1967, over 215 ships visited Subic Bay each month. Many of these ships were military sea transportation service ships, which bore the designation "USNS" rather than "USS," bringing over 45,000 tons of food, ammunition, and supplies and over two million barrels of fuel oil, aviation gasoline, and JP-4 jet fuel each month, including fuels transferred to Clark Air Base via a forty-one-mile pipeline. The Naval Supply Depot maintained an inventory of 200,000 parts. More than 4,000,000 sailors visiting Subic Bay in 1967 purchased more than $25 million in duty-free goods from the navy exchange.

During a Westpac deployment, Subic Bay usually served as a hub for operations for ships like the *Bob E.* During a six-month deployment, a ship would typically replenish and make repairs in Subic Bay five or six times. Consequently, of all the ports used by the US Navy, sailors spent the most time on liberty in Subic. Olongapo City was just outside the gates of Subic Bay, and because of the large number of sailors and marines who passed through Subic Bay, an entire liberty entertainment industry flourished. The city boasted hundreds of bars, most with live music at night, and each had its own private prostitution service, with the variety and types of sexual service available differing from bar to bar. The girls in the bars, in addition to providing sex, offered much-needed companionship, dance partners, and female conversation, as long as a sailor was willing to "buy a girl a drink," which usually consisted of very expensive bourbon, which smelled quite a bit like tea. The companionship lasted as long as the sailor was willing to continue to buy drinks. Pretty much everyone knew the gambit, but lonely sailors on liberty were more than willing to be complicit in the sham in exchange for the companionship. At the end of the night, the sailor could buy the girl out of the bar, and she was his, not only for that night, but each time the sailor visited the bar, which encouraged loyalty from the bar's customers.

In addition to the bars, there were a multitude of massage parlors, where the primary focus was on the *full-frontal* massage. Restaurants, barbers, street vendors, and people in alleys cooking great-smelling, unidentifiable barbecue on hibachis made for a colorful, dangerous feeling of adventure on liberty. Bert loved to eat the food from these vendors, as long as he didn't know what kind of meat it was, and the vendors were happy to simply smile, hand over great meat on a stick, and accept their peso or two charge.

Subic Bay was one of three naval bases in the Pacific with a naval communications station to turn the communications duties over to. For the radiomen, this meant they would have more liberty in Subic Bay than any other port they would visit. Once in port, the communications duties belonged to the communications station, and other than regular shipboard duties, the radiomen could feast on some relief from port and starboard watches.

As the senior enlisted man in OC division, B.S. took it upon himself to provide each new radioman and signalman with his first "orientation" to Olongapo, so that he could learn the rules of engagement in the city; build some skills to avoid being mugged, robbed, killed, or arrested while in town; and get to know B.S.'s favorite bars, massage parlors, and tattoo shops. B.S. was famous throughout the ship for the amazing array of pornographic and mesmerizing tattoos, including a fly he had tattooed on the tip of his manhood, which, if plied with enough alcohol, B.S. was more than willing to display.

Once the ship was docked and the variety of tasks required to transition the ship to shore power, water, and sewer services were completed, a general call for liberty was given over the ship's PA system. B.S. grabbed Bert by the neck and told him they were going to stop off at the chief's club for a "quick drink" before they headed out in town. Although Bert wasn't officially allowed in the chief's club, B.S. was a legend in Subic Bay, and nobody ever questioned him dragging a young sailor in for a drink. At the table, a pretty young waitress came over and gave B.S. a big hug. "You no come for long time, Boggs!" said the waitress.

"Yeah, sweetie, but I'm *coming* tonight!" replied B.S. with a wink and a slap on her behind. "Okay, so bring two shots of rum, two Singapore slings, and two beers." B.S. then looked up at Bert and said, "What will you have?"

Bert, a bit dismayed that this was B.S.'s idea of stopping for a "quick drink," ordered a beer and then sat and watched B.S. inhale the drinks in the time it took Bert to drink about half of his beer. "We better get moving," B.S. growled as he pushed back his chair. "My town is waiting!"

Bert and B.S. walked out of the club, down Magsaysay Drive, and out of the main gate of the naval base and crossed a narrow bridge over a rather smelly river. In the river were children in small canoes, begging for money. B.S. threw down some money, and the children dove into the river to retrieve it. Bert could only think that this river, officially dubbed the "Shit" River by sailors, was, in fact, used for that purpose. As Bert looked out on the river, he saw on its banks hundreds of "houses" made of corrugated metal, with dirt floors, no doors, and windows simply cut into the metal without glass. People came and went from these houses and washed in the river, and their drinking water source was rain barrels next to their houses. Bert had come from a very small town and had never seen anything really resembling poverty before. His mouth gaping open, he realized that the people of this country were beyond any kind of poverty that had ever been described to him. He was stunned by the way these people had to live and saddened that people lived with such impecuniousness.

Shaken out of his shock, Bert followed B.S. to the first stop on the journey, which was the money exchange. "Here's where we buy our circus tickets!" B.S. chuckled as though he had coined that phrase. They exchanged their money for Philippine pesos and proceeded down the street, followed by a throng of begging children. Past the bridge, Magsaysay Drive continued as the main road to entertainment in Olongapo. Bert was enthralled with the sights and smells of Magsaysay Drive, which was bustling with sailors, marines, pedestrians, jeepneys, motor scooters, and bicycles everywhere. Jeepneys, along with three-wheeled motor scooters with cabs, were a primary form of public transportation in the Philippines. Most were old and highly modified Willys Jeeps, left behind when America withdrew from the Philippines at the end of World War II. The jeepneys were customized to carry more passengers, and Bert saw that no two looked the same, each one decorated with multiple bright colors, chrome and cloth awnings with tassels hanging down, and, of course, the obligatory statue of Jesus or the driver's favorite saint on the dashboard. Each jeepney driver competed with the others for the flashiest and gaudiest jeepney possible, which created a palette of colors whizzing loudly down the streets.

What also lined Magsaysay Drive were countless street vendors, bars, restaurants, shops, and night spots, another paradise on earth for sailors. Bert could hear live music coming from each bar out in the street. It was amazing the variety of musical genres. Chicago would be coming from one bar, Janis Joplin from the next, and then Johnny Cash the following. Each bar had a live band, and each sounded amazingly like the actual performer. When Bert would poke his head into a bar to see who the performer was, he was always met with the sight of a short, thin Filipino playing proficiently, mimicking the performer of choice.

The evening proceeded much like the stories Bert had been hearing for weeks from the sailors. Each sailor had his own version of some amazing adventure involving hookers, alcohol, and some kind of trouble that he barely escaped. Bert heard many of these stories multiple times, and the amazing thing was that each time the story was retold, the adventure (or misadventure) grew in proportion and color. Bert had quickly learned that telling "sea stories" was a favorite pastime of the sailors, each trying to outdo the others with bigger and more colorful stories, most of which had some basis in a long-exaggerated truth. It occurred to Bert that the stories were remarkably similar to the fishing stories that his uncle used to tell but with sex and booze. It was widely accepted among sailors that a basic story could be exaggerated to the point of complete fabrication, with all of the participants in agreement that the story was, in fact, how it actually happened.

"And if you think Olongapo is amazing, wait until we get to Subic City! That's where Marilyn's Number One is, and down the street is the Texas club," mused Pigman. "They have a pond out in front with a wrought-iron-type fence around the water. They've got live crocodiles about in there. There's a lady with a basket that will sell you a live baby chicken. Once you get your baby chicken, you can toss it in the pond for the crocodiles to eat! But let me tell you what. B.S. went one step further. He bit the head off the baby chick and threw it in!" Of course, Bert never substantiated the truth of this story, but it didn't matter to the others as they all sat guzzling beers and nodding at Pigman's story.

As Bert witnessed this foreign experience, he had difficulty believing such a place could even exist. Although it was fascinating, Bert's mind kept going back to the poverty he had seen along the Shit River, and as he looked at the bartenders, hookers, street vendors, and children on the street, he realized that they were all doing these jobs because they had to in order to survive, not as a matter of choice.

As the evening wore on, Bert began to become increasingly anxious about B.S.'s dentures. The more alcohol B.S. ingested, the more he complained about the dentures, and the more he fiddled with them, regularly popping them in and out of his mouth. As the night was wearing down, B.S. got up to go use the head. When he returned, there were no dentures. No dentures! Bert jumped up and ran into the head, only to find them thrown in the trash. Putting them in his pocket, he decided it would be best to return them in the morning when B.S.'s blood alcohol level would be slightly lower.

The evening wore on with women doing unnatural things on their tables, numerous topless women, and a substantial amount of drinking. Because the Philippines was under the control of Ferdinand Marcos, a despotic dictator, the country had been under martial law for years. The biggest effect on the sailors was that one either had to have a room, be in a hooker's home, or be back on base by midnight. Rumors abounded of drunk sailors being rounded up, jailed, and held for small bribes until navy officials could get them out. For Bert, this didn't matter so much tonight, as his radio watch started at midnight, and he was on what sailors called "Cinderella Liberty," which meant he was required to be back on the ship before midnight to work.

The next day, Bert was given two days of what the navy called "R&R," which was a military acronym for "rest and relaxation" and which B.S. called "I&I" (intercourse and intoxication). This meant that he, Lucky, Wonder, Pigman, Shroom, and Red would be able to get out of the city to see the sights. Several people suggested a trip to Baggio, which was a small village in the mountains that was a tourist town and a good place to get wooden carvings and other handcrafts as souvenirs. Wonder was having none of that. They were going to Subic City, the wild west of the Philippines.

After the six adventurers had stopped at the ritual money exchange for their circus tickets and jumped on a jeepney, Wonder leaned over to Bert with words of advice for the day. "Listen to me, Bert. Subic City is crazy, and it's really easy to get yourself into a load of trouble. So, I want you to do everything I tell you to do —*everything*, without hesitation and without question. Understood?"

Bert could barely manage a grunt, but looking into the serious-ness of Wonder's eyes, he gave him a very slow, very large nod. The jeepney gradually left the hustle-bustle of Olongapo City, and they followed a beautiful coastline about a half an hour to Subic City.

Subic City was smaller and much quieter than Olongapo, and as they came into town, Bert saw the sign for "Marilyn's #1." They stopped there and crossed the street. "Ah, home sweet home!" declared Wonder, followed by a bunch of rebel yells from the others as they walked in the door of their favorite Subic City bar, "Texas."

The bar was much different from the bars in Olongapo. This one had windows and a magnificent view of the beach and the ocean. But madness was palpable immediately. Women were everywhere. Five of them sat down with the adventurers. Shroom was sitting next to Bert, and a girl sat on Shroom's lap and immediately pulled off her top.

"Lucy!" Shroom shouted. "So nice to see them again!"

The guys obviously had prior relationships with all the girls who sat down, as each of the girls knew their names and vice versa. An older Filipino man came rushing over. "Mr. Wonder! Mr. Shroom! So good to see you boys again!"

"Vedasto!" everyone shouted at once. "We're home!"

Wonder signaled the man over to his side. "Vedasto, this is Bert. It's his first time here. I want you to treat him well, and I want you to give him your best girl, if you know what I mean, and I'm paying for everything."

"No problem, Mr. Wonder! I have just the girl for him!" And with a simple hand signal from him, a beautiful young woman appeared. "This is Vilma, Mr. Bert. She will take very, very good care of you!"

As Vilma sat down, Wonder leaned over again and whispered into Bert's ear, "Vilma has a reputation for being extraordinary in her skills, Bert. I want you to do *everything* she tells you to do, without question." Bert had not even decided if he was going to take part in exposing himself to the sex offered seemingly everywhere he went these days. Especially after seeing the poverty in town, he felt as though he would be wrongfully taking advantage of another human who had little choice in the matter. Yet, as a nineteen-year-old virgin with three beers and four glasses of some mysterious sweet drink in him, it didn't take long for him to place his misgivings away.

The five guys were having a great time drinking, singing, and willingly accepting the compensated flirtations of the women at the table. Various vendors came to the table taking pictures and selling trinkets. Bert bought a great pickpocket-proof watchband. This was a "must" here, as pickpockets abounded. Bert had lost his watch the first night of liberty to a six-year-old pickpocket and didn't want that to happen again. The drinking and the laughing grew louder as the blood alcohol levels rose. And then with a "hell yes!" Shroom spotted a vendor he had obviously been waiting for. He jumped up, waved, and shouted at the vendor, who immediately came to the table. "Bert!" exclaimed Shroom. "Meet the balut vendor! This is your chance to collect on the bet!"

A sinking feeling came over Bert as the vendor opened a basket full of very large gray eggs. The vendor indicated they cost one peso, so, with an already rising sense of nausea, he exchanged his peso for the egg. Everyone at the table came to a hush.

"You're not actually thinking of eating that, are you, Bert?" said Red.

"I'm not sure how to eat it," Bert openly pondered.

Although none of the people at the table had taken the opportunity to try one, they all knew exactly what to do. "It's simple, man," Shroom said. "You just crack off the top and slug it down. Before you do, we are going to get back because man those little motherfuckers stink. Just slug it down, and try not to think about the smell or the crunchy little beak and bones or the slick, snotty stuff in between."

Bert knew that this was his opportunity to prove himself and, not forgetting the bet for the *everything included* massage at Marilyn's #1, took a deep breath, cracked off the top, and without a second of hesitation, slugged it back like a shot of tequila. Although his brain was screaming and his stomach was crying not to torture it in this way (and his brain was telling him he was crazy), he ate it without retching, without making a face, and even smiled and licked out the inside of the shell. "Not bad," Bert stated with unaccustomed confidence. "Might just have another in a bit."

The shipmates and the table went into a frenzy of cheers, and Shroom came over and gave Bert a big hug. "We're going tomorrow for an everything-included massage, man! But in the meantime, don't breathe on me, dude. You reek!"

Bert woke up the next morning next to Vilma, completely unable to remember leaving the bar, getting a room, or anything that happened after that, although based on the fact that neither had clothes on, he guessed that he must have lost his virginity somewhere in the night. Bert immediately felt three things at the same time. First, he was excited that he was no longer a virgin and was now a "man"; second, he was ashamed that he had taken advantage of a woman who only consented to sex because she had no other choices in life; and third, he felt a tingle in his privates, which he immediately feared was the clap.

The ride back from Subic City that afternoon was troubling for Bert. As they approached the streets of Olongapo City, he really *noticed* the children on the streets in detail for the first time. Particularly, he noticed how many of them were obviously mixed-race—blue-eyed, brown-skinned children; children with curly black hair; children with light complexions and blond hair. Few of them looked like Filipinos, all legacies of the sailors and marines who had visited Olongapo and done exactly what he had. Bert was suddenly filled with shame that he had participated in something like this and swiftly started worrying that he might, like the thousands of others who had come before him, have left behind a living being, whom he would never know and could never care for. Bert immediately resolved three things. First, he would never have sex in this place again; second, he would find a way to pay back his mistake; and third, he would see the doc as soon as he got back to the ship to check for venereal disease.

As he approached the *Peckham*, Bert saw Lucky dragging himself back, also, after what was obviously a night that involved plenty of booze and very little sleep.

"Hey, Bert," said Lucky. "I need a favor from you, but believe me, it will pay off in spades for you, man."

"Anything, buddy," Bert said.

"I need you to give me three hours of unlimited access to the MARS phone on the ship."

Bert gave him a questioning look. The MARS, which stood for the military auxiliary radio system, was a program sponsored by the Department of Defense that created a civilian auxiliary mostly made up primarily of licensed amateur radio operators who were interested in assisting the military with their communications. Long-distance calls from overseas, when possible, were impossibly expensive and could not be accomplished from the oceans. Through the MARS stations, the radio shack could set up something similar to a telephone system for people to call home in emergencies, and the ship's officers often gave phone calls as rewards to sailors for being squared-away. It wasn't quite a phone, as it was transmitted over HF transmitters and went through a HAM operator who had to manually switch the sides of a communication. It was rather annoying to say "over" each time you were done with a thought, but that gave the radio operator the key to switch the mode so that the other person could speak. Because of the distance, the quality could be poor, but for sailors missing their families, poor communication was better than none.

"It's going to benefit you, Bert, I promise, but I need to make some calls to put some deals together."

"Fine, Lucky," Bert said, "but we'll have to do this covertly. You aren't even allowed in the radio shack, so we'll have to sneak you in when there's nobody around to object."

Over the course of the next few days, Lucky made over three hours of MARS phone calls, which were not simple for Bert to orchestrate covertly. But when Lucky emerged after the last call, he slapped Bert on the back and said, "You are going to like this!"

Coming out of his daydream about the past, Bert's attention was brought back to the jungle as he came upon one of his snares that actually had something in it! He was elated to see a snake, about four feet long, writhing in his snare. With some care, not knowing if the snake was venomous or not, Bert killed it, skinned it, and used two of his last three matches lighting a small fire on which to cook his prey. Luck was with him this morning. It was the first dry morning of his three-day ordeal, and he managed to build a reasonably good fire. After putting the snake on a stick, he roasted it and without any reservation, ate the finest meal of his life. The snake offered Bert some energy, which had been lacking, and gave him a newfound focus on navigating to his rendezvous point, which would be his means of hopefully leaving the jungle behind forever.

10

SEMPER FEE FI FO

G unnery Sergeant Huckins was distinctly uncomfortable. He was even getting grouchy. During his entire tenure in the Marine Corps, he had never seen such a lackadaisical, ill-disciplined platoon of marines. It wasn't just that he was dogmatic about marine discipline; he understood that once discipline diminished, marines were subject to a danger much greater than any outside enemy. They not only became less prepared for any eventuality of combat, but they began seeing themselves less as a unit of marines and more like individuals, which meant they were subject to the same disunity that the outside world had fallen into. Huck worried that the lives of good marines would be jeopardized because of the relaxation of important standards, and this feeling grew inside of him every day.

Huck had approached Manny several times, imploring more discipline and a more regimented approach to their days on Squid Island. Manny had consented to increased physical training, increased military training, and more days in which the marines would uniform up to look and act like marines, which were all good to Huck, yet Huck couldn't abide Manny trying to be "one of the guys" and playing volleyball with the men, having meals with the men, and giving the men plenty of time off for swimming, volleyball, and leisure activities.

Huck had grown up with Marine Corps blood. His father had been a career marine, and Huck had spent his childhood living on military bases, going to military schools, and being raised with a father who lived marine discipline both at work and at home. Unlike most of his friends, Huck never resented being a military "brat" and resolved at the age of twelve to enlist in the marines the day he was legally allowed to do so. Huck was a "lifer," a term for those who are career military, and he never gave a different life a second thought. He was happiest on deployment and had seen action as he volunteered for two tours in Vietnam. Huck considered himself a professional, and the Marine Corps principles were the ones he lived, to the greatest extent possible, throughout every corner of his life.

One afternoon, Huck's worries about discipline on Squid Island were confirmed when two platoon riflemen got into a coconut fight with each other over who was going to get the use of the "throne hammock," the one good hammock they had which was tied between two beautiful trees in a shady part of the beach. The throne hammock was a much-coveted nap location and was subject to multiple conflicts among the men over who had a right to use the throne. This time, however, the conflict became aggressive when coconuts became weapons of mass bruising. As the fight escalated, one of the marines was knocked unconscious, and the other found his nose split open to the cheek. To make matters worse, none of their fellow marines tried to break up the fight, instead betting on who would be the winner.

With great dismay in his voice, Huck implored Manny to reconsider his notions of discipline on the island. "LT, this is what happens when we stop acting like marines," implored Huck.

"I know it doesn't look good, Gunny, but fights are bound to happen among a bunch of nineteen- and twenty-year-olds with testosterone flooding their systems."

"It's more than that, sir," implored Huck. "We need more discipline, and we need to act more like marines."

Manny simply shook his head. "I understand your position, Gunny, but keep in mind that we'll be getting orders to ship back home within days, and we won't have to worry about any of this. Why not let these kids have some relaxation?"

Huck silently remembered the conversations he had had with Lieutenant Kirschoff over the past months, and Manny's mantra was always that they would be getting orders home "any day" for the past four months. Orders had yet to come. Being a good marine meant following orders, however, and so Huck decided he would lessen the pressure he was putting on the LT and, instead, privately work with the platoon without raising the LT's concern. The LT had not ordered him to back down. He had simply *not* given orders to increase drill and discipline. Huck could work with that.

Without drawing much attention to the changes, Huck began instituting a more rigorous physical training program and made some "suggestions" to his men that uniforms needed to be paid attention to. When the gunnery sergeant suggests something, most marines consider that to be an order, and as such, the marines started looking and acting, once again, as marines. Manny was supportive of the changes, and marine discipline gradually returned to the platoon.

11

THE LFDT

Rear Admiral Ira Stephens was quite proud of the changes that he had effected during his tenure as chief of naval operations. Along with "modernizing" uniforms and restoring the beard policy in the navy, Ira's pet project was something that he called the "landing force deployment team." He unveiled his concept of the LFDT at the weekly meeting of the navy command in Washington DC in late 1974.

"Imagine this scenario," Ira began. "We have special operations teams with the SEALS, but we have only eight teams worldwide. We have marines who are highly trained in combat, assault, and defense missions, but they are on bases scattered throughout the world. We have none of these in the places that are the most mobile and closest to emergencies: our surface fleet.

"Oh yes, there are usually trained people onboard a destroyer who can use an M16, shotgun, or grenade launcher, but they have no training in infiltration, defense, or rescue operations," explained the CNO. "If there is a hostage crisis in Malaysia or American Samoa or the Marianas, it would take days, perhaps even a week or two, in order for our special forces or marines to reach those destinations. And yet, we have naval destroyers and frigates scattered throughout the world, most within hours or a couple of days, tops, to reach those places. As such, I propose that we create a model team onboard every naval destroyer and frigate, consisting of twelve to fifteen men who, in addition to their regular jobs, have very specific training in 'light' tactical operations."

The admirals, their staff, and others at the table were noticeably uncomfortable. Admiral Johnson, Commander of the Third Fleet, was white and shaking. "You can't possibly expect that a bunch of fat, out-of-shape sailors on some lone destroyer in the Pacific could ever have the skills to accomplish anything other than getting themselves killed? Do you, Ira?"

Ira Stephens placed both hands on the table and stared straight into the face of the second most senior naval officer in the US Navy and said, "That is exactly what we are going to do. Of course, we'll have to create several test groups. I propose that we take five ships and recruit fifteen or so volunteers on these ships to go through four months of intense training. We already have training in place. We'll send them to an abbreviated SEAL school, marine combat school, and, for those who are adept, sniper school. We'll train them in combat arms and give them the basic skills we give our combat troops so that they will *not* be a bunch of fat, out-of-shape sailors who will get themselves killed but will be a highly specialized strike force, in case there are no other options. And there will be no further discussion on this. You are all hereby ordered to create five completely trained LFDTs ready to go within five months."

And with that, the LFDT came into existence. The plan was to recruit only volunteers from ships that would include gunner's mates, as they were already trained in things that blew up; a hospital corpsman, which every destroyer had onboard; a radioman, which every ship also had; and several ambitious closet special forces wannabes to round things out. They would spend a few weeks in basic combat school, a few weeks in SEAL school, and a few weeks in marine combat school, and two who showed promise would also spend three weeks in sniper school. Each would attend the navy's POW training camp and jungle warfare school in Subic Bay, Philippines. Anyone who has attended any of these schools knows that such a condensed version of highly skilled training is practically impossible, a fact that Rear Admiral Ira Stephens did not. Five Knox-class frigates were chosen for the test as, unlike destroyers, they had helicopter pads and hangars that could easily transport the LFDT members off the ship and into whatever hotspot they were called upon to occupy.

Bert remembered the day that the *Bob E.* was selected to be one of those five ships, as he received the message in the radio shack and delivered it to the captain. He kept an eye on the progress, and recruiting seemed easy at first, as the gunner's mates on the ship were mostly people who would have rather been special forces anyway but had mostly failed the physical or mental entrance tests for that career path. The *Peckham* had two hospital corpsmen, one of whom had served with a marine battalion in Vietnam, so he was persuaded to "volunteer." By the end of the second week of the recruitment phase, the *Peckham* only had one spot remaining, and it was a special spot. They needed a radioman to round out their team, and nobody—but *nobody*—in communications division had the least desire to be a part of this setup.

Bert clearly remembered the conversation that took place in the radio shack as the recruiting call went out for a radioman to join the LFDT. "I joined the navy because I wanted to take my bed with me when I went into combat!" shouted Red to the rest of the radio team. Red was the most senior radioman onboard. "And shit, I'm so fat that if I look down naked, I can't tell what sex I am. I'd die the first day of training.

"Besides that, and more importantly, do you have any idea what the life span of a radioman in combat is?" Red paused and replaced the intense, stony look on his face with a much softer one. "You probably got the lecture in Radioman 'A' School. The average life span of a radioman in combat is five fucking minutes. Why? Well, just imagine the scenario. You are wearing a combat radio on your back, which with the crypto gear weighs almost sixty pounds, so you are the slowest person on the team. In addition, you are carrying the same weapons everyone else is while at the same time trying to stay in contact with command. I can't fart and chew bubble gum at the same time, much less focus on communicating and not getting my head shot off. If that isn't enough, you have a huge six-foot antenna waving at the enemy, coming out of your radio, which advertises the words, *Shoot me! I'm a radioman!* If that *really* isn't enough, you are always right next to the commanding officer, as you are the one relaying messages between command and your team leader. The enemy isn't stupid. They know that where that antenna goes, so goes the biggest target on the team. So, my opinion, you would have to be absolutely fucking stupid to volunteer for that job. Just my opinion and you know that opinions are like assholes: everybody has one, and they all smell."

With that stirring recruiting lecture, the consensus in the radio shack was cast. The captain even made a trip to the radio shack to give a pep talk and recruiting pitch, which lacked the veracity of Red's experienced opinion. With a great deal of dismay, the ship's leadership began looking for alternatives. The reputation of Captain Stilton and his ship rode on finding their last LFDT member, and it didn't look good that they could fill the radioman slot, as the CNO had mandated it be an "all-volunteer" team.

Having finished his gourmet meal of roast snake, Bert focused on his last task of the three days of hell in the jungle: get to the rendezvous point by 1300 hours. During the training he had received over the past eight weeks, he had learned land navigation. Prior to being dropped off in the jungle for this final test, he had also learned how to navigate in covered jungles where there are no reference points. He hoped he had the skills necessary to accomplish this final task, and he had never wanted anything more than to get the hell out of this nasty place. As he made his way in the direction of the LZ, he hoped he would find an awaiting helicopter. Bert thought back to the events that had led him there.

12

OF MICE AND DENTURES

To say that Bert was enjoying deployment was a complete understatement. While the work hours were long, there was always time to go above deck and look out on the magnificent ocean. Bert simply could not get enough of the sounds and smells the sea provided, and whenever he was able, he went out to see the sunsets. The sunsets in the middle of the ocean were spectacular. It was easy to see how large the world was from the deck of a ship in which the ocean expanded everywhere and was the only thing, other than the sky, one could see.

One evening, the seas were as calm as he had ever seen them. As the sun began to set, the captain must have recognized the unusually calm seas and extraordinarily beautiful reds, yellows, oranges, and magentas wrapped in the palette in front of their eyes. Commander Stilton brought the ship to a full stop, and as other sailors joined Bert on the signal bridge, the glass-calm ocean looked like a giant, unmoving mirror of color. The sea was so calm they could see sea snakes swimming on the surface. As Bert was drinking in the beauty of the scene, without warning, a group of a dozen dolphins appeared from the depths, apparently recognizing the state of the ocean also. As the ship stopped in the midst of the ocean, the dolphins began a celebratory performance exceeding anything at any marine park in the world, as they jumped, flipped, chirped, and swam in a performance that felt as though it was sent from King Neptune himself, just for the pleasure of the sailors on the *Bob E.*, Bert thought to himself that he would never, ever see anything as spectacular in the rest of his life.

Once the show was over and the ship was once again underway, Lucky came up to Bert with a broad smile on his face. "I have your printer all worked out, Bert, my man," he chirped, with a combination of braggadocio and exuberance.

"How in the hell did you do that?" a shocked Bert hooted.

"Well, I don't actually have it yet, Bert, because it's going to require you to come up with something for me to use. It's a complicated deal I've put together." Bert stood in stunned silence as Lucky explained the amazingly intricate serious of deals that would be required to accomplish this, apparently the outcome of all the MARS calls that he had made. "So, the radiomen on the *Ashtabula* have an extra printer they are willing to give up," said Lucky. The USS *Ashtabula* was a destroyer tender, also based in Pearl Harbor, which served as a sort of floating repair shop. Although navy ships carry a complement of people highly capable of making many of the repairs necessary, sometimes certain equipment, parts, or expertise are required that are not on the ship. The *Ashtabula* patrolled along with other ships, and when called upon to help a disabled ship or repair a radar or something complicated, they were available in places that shipyard facilities were not.

"Great!" said Bert. "They are going to be in Subic when we're there. We can get it then!"

"Not so fast, big guy," cautioned Lucky. "They want something in exchange. They want their own film projector and ten movies. Now, I know what you're thinking, impossible, right? Well, it just happens that I know the chief who runs the submarine base theater in Pearl. He's kind of a movie collector and has exactly what they need. Unfortunately, he wanted to trade for a new Martin guitar. I know the guys in the band at the enlisted club, and they are willing to trade a Martin for plane tickets to their home in Texas for a vacation. So, I'm thinking, where can I get those? So, I called out to a staff sergeant at Hickam Air Force Base I know, and he's willing to get them spots on a MAC plane, in exchange for forty pounds of coffee. I talked to Chief Masters, the head of our mess decks onboard, and he's got extra coffee he'll trade."

"Wow, that's amazing," said Bert. "But I'm sure he wants something, too, right?"

"Exactly," replied Lucky. "That's where you come in."

"Me? What do I have to trade?"

"Just so happens Chief Masters has a family back in Pearl, and he'd like to be able to call home once a week while we're on deployment, to talk to his wife and kids. You have the MARS station up and running, so, voila, you let him call home once a week while we're on deployment, and you got your printer."

Bert looked stunned and confused. "How in the hell did you manage all this from here, and how do you keep track of all that?"

"All those phone calls you let me make the other day, I put to good use. And I've made deals with all of them before, so they trust me." Many times, after he lost touch with Lucky, Bert often wondered if Lucky had become a commodities trader or a diplomat. Whatever became of Lucky, Bert was the beneficiary of a great deal of effort, and from then on, Lucky drank on Bert's ticket whenever they went out together.

Continuing deployment meant periods of training and patrolling off the South China Sea and the Indian Ocean, along with at-sea refueling and re-provisioning when massive supply ships would come alongside the *Bob E.* while they were underway out in the middle of the ocean, shoot lines across as they matched one another's speeds, refuel, and send pallets of food, supplies, and the most coveted prize, mail, across those lines to the *Bob E.*, so they could remain at sea during patrols.

Although there were many days underway with nothing to see but ocean in every direction, the long times at sea were rewarded with stops at exotic ports of call, such as Singapore, American Samoa,

and Mombasa, Kenya, and such less than exotic but enjoyable locations as Yokosuka, Japan, and Pusan, Korea, each with adventures of
its own. Prior to entering any port, an officer would give lectures on
places in the cities to include, sights to see, customs that were necessary to know, and, most important, places that were off-limits to
sailors. The sailors paid great attention to these notifications so that
they could plan where to spend their liberty time. Bert never imagined so many places with so much prostitution and alcohol and so
many souvenirs for sale.

Interspersed with exotic locations were regular stops in Subic Bay,
and Bert gradually found his favorite places to eat, drink, and be
merry. In addition, rather than taking advantage of the sexual opportunities, Bert spent many of his days off at St. Joseph's Catholic
Church orphanage assuaging his guilt and helping to repair the
orphanage, which was overflowing with what Bert learned were
called "Amerasian" children, who were relegated to being accepted
neither by their own people in the Philippines nor by the people in
the United States. Bert's guilt was only increased by this knowledge.
His trip to the sick bay showed no signs of venereal disease, but the
creepy feelings in his organs caused him to revisit sickbay on a
regular basis, as he was certain Doc had missed some rare, awful
form of clap. Finally, in exasperation, the Doc gave Bert a shot of
penicillin just to get rid of him.

As the deployment began to draw to an end, Subic Bay would be
the last stop prior to heading home to Pearl Harbor. The crew had
four days to reprovision the ship and satiate their taste for Olongapo
life prior to heading back to the real world. Bert was proud and
relieved that while he had had to rescue B.S.'s dentures from the trash
twice and from a street gutter once and purchase them from a hooker
at the Wild West #1 club, it looked like B.S.'s dentures would return
safely home, and he would not have to suffer Adelle's wrath.

The final night in Subic Bay was a big one. The communications
gang gathered at Wild West #1 for a farewell party that included cases
of San Miguel beer and gallons of a strange concoction called "Mojo"
that contained, among other things, 151 proof rum, Everclear, beer,

pineapple juice, and Hawaiian punch. Bert thought it was about the best thing he had ever tasted, and the funny part of the drink was that he didn't feel drunk after drinking it—until he tried to stand.

B.S. was in rare form that night, telling sea stories with the best of them. As he regaled them with hair-raising stories of debauchery and near-death experiences, Bert kept close watch on the dentures, and although B.S. complained about them several times, he didn't show signs of losing them. At one point in the celebration, a Navy SEAL came into the bar. It was a pretty simple matter to identify a SEAL, even in civvies, mostly from the huge biceps, lack of neck, and swagger. This guy was particularly drunk, and as he walked in, he stopped at each table, staring in an almost mesmerized fashion at each person at each table. Finally, he stood up on the bar and screamed, "Can I have your attention, you assholes? There ain't a motherfucker leaving this bar who doesn't fight me first tonight!"

Wonder shouted back, "I'm good!" and the group raised a glass in resolve that this was their hangout until the SEAL got bored or passed out.

As the group began walking back to base shortly before midnight, B.S. was complaining loudly about his dentures. Bert kept a close watch on him, as they could go flying at any moment, and each time B.S.'s hand went near his mouth, Bert readied himself for action. Bert was thankful, as they came aboard the *Bob E.*, that B.S.'s choppers remained in his mouth. As everyone was safely aboard, Bert breathed a huge sigh of relief.

Many people who have been through significant traumatic events say they remember the event happening in slow motion. Slow motion is exactly how Bert would remember the events of the next few minutes. He watched as B.S. calmly staggered to the edge of the fantail of the ship, looked out over into Subic Bay, reached into his mouth, pulled out his teeth, and gave them a hall-of-fame baseball outfielder-worthy toss right into Subic Bay. With a scream of sheer panic, Bert ran to the fantail. He remembered marveling that the choppers weren't sinking. They were just floating on the surface, and he could see them, about twenty feet away. Without thinking, Bert pulled off his shoes and prepared for a dive into the reeking harbor, only to be grabbed by the officer of the deck. Looking into the face of the OOD, he saw, staring back at him, none other than LTJG Hudson. Bert gave Rock a pleading, begging look, but the officer was having none of it. A sinking feeling came to Bert as Rock snarled, "Don't even think about going in after them, Bertram. Do so and you will experience my wrath. That, I promise!"

"But I have to! I swore an oath to B.S.'s wife not to let him lose them!" Bert choked out.

"Ain't fucking happening on my watch, sailor."

Bert turned back toward the quarterdeck, dismayed and heartbroken that he had let Adelle and B.S. down. All he could see in his mind was the grief-ridden, disappointed face Adelle would have when she learned the news of the loss of the dentures. It was simply too much for Bert to bear. *I must think of something*, thought Bert. It was at that moment that he passed a sound-powered phone and had what at the time in his alcohol-saturated brain was a *genius* idea. He ran to the far side of the quarterdeck, called on the phone over to Rock on the other side of the quarterdeck, and when he answered, in a meager attempt to deepen and disguise his voice, Bert shouted, "There's race riot that has broken out on the mess decks!" with as deep a voice as possible. "We need help ASAP!"

Rock, looking like John Wayne leading the cavalry into battle, drew his pistol and took off for the mess decks, which left only the deck watch outside, along with Bert's shipmates. Bert could still see the semibuoyant choppers gradually sinking in the harbor, and with one giant leap for sailor-kind, Bert dove into the noxious waters of Subic Bay. It took him three surface dives, but he came up with the teeth, waving them above his head to the others. Cheers, applause, and screams of victory came from Bert's shipmates. Bert swam to a ladder on the pier and as he looked up, gazed into the face of Rock, with two sentries, weapons drawn.

As morning broke, the three familiar blows of the ship's horn indicated the *Bob E.* was once again underway. Red stood above Bert, shaking his head. "Bert, you are in a shitload of trouble, man," he said with a look of grief in his eyes. "Leaving the ship without permission, making a false report of a race riot, and of all people in the world, lying to force Rock to abandon his watch. It would have gone badly with anyone but Rock? He already hated you. I don't know, but you might be facing a court-martial. You know those three stripes on your sleeve. You'll definitely be kissing them goodbye."

"I know," said Bert sadly, "but it had to be done. I couldn't let Adelle down."

"I don't think the Skipper is going to consider that a valid exoneration, man," said Shroom. "But it was totally cool, dude," he added with gusto. "You're like a legend on the ship, man." Although it was nice to hear, the praise was little consolation for the events Bert knew were looming in his near future. Shroom concluded by looking down and saying with dismal quietness, "I think you're fucked too, man."

The navy has a variety of ways to discipline its sailors, depending upon the situation and the severity of the "crime." Court-martial under the Uniform Code of Military Justice (UCMJ) was usually reserved for the more severe crimes, as it is a criminal trial with lawyers, judges, evidence, and such. Punishments under court-martial can vary between dishonorable discharge, time in the brig (navy jail), and confinement in a military prison. They generally take months to conclude while the service member usually sits in jail. In addition to court-martial, captains of ships have been given unique jurisdiction for many infractions, usually relatively minor. This method of dispensing justice has traditionally been important because ships historically have been alone at sea for many weeks or months. Captain's Mast is considered "nonjudicial" because the captain has no real rules about how to conduct a hearing and wide discretion about how to punish.

Captain's Mast was set for the next day, as the captain wanted to get things over with quickly. It was good news that it sounded like Bert wasn't going to be held for court-martial, but the cloud of misfortune loomed over his head, almost visibly. Bert dressed in his dress blues for the hearing and appeared, along with B.S. and Red, at the captain's stateroom ahead of time.

"I'll put in a good word for you, son," B.S. slowly said, teeth firmly intact in his mouth. "That'll count for something and, hey, been there four times myself. It ain't so fucking bad." Small consolation for Bert but good that B.S. was willing to speak for him.

At the appointed time, the three walked into the captain's stateroom. Captain Stilton was with his executive officer, LT Commander Hawthorne, and LTJG Hudson, primary witness for the prosecution. Both the CO and the XO had extremely solemn looks on their faces, much as one would expect to see on the face of a judge sentencing a man to death. Rock had a look of sheer pleasure and amusement on his face.

Captain Stilton was highly regarded on the *Bob E*. He was a lifelong bachelor and was not a graduate of the Naval Academy. In fact, he had graduated from the Merchant Marine Academy and had served as a merchant marine for several years before joining the navy. Because he was a bachelor, he had no family to be concerned about being away from for long periods of time, and among the sailors on the *Bob E*. who were also single, it was good news, as Captain Stilton volunteered at every opportunity to get underway. That meant lots of time on deployments to great ports of call. Captain Stilton was known to jump into a helicopter deck basketball game with the enlisted men and was never terrifically formal about his position, at least to the extent allowed by tradition and decorum. It had been for hundreds of years a tradition that when the captain of a ship entered a room, the senior enlisted or officer would shout, "Captain on Deck" or "Attention on Deck," and all hands stood at attention. Stilton was uncomfortable with this formality and so was free with "At ease, men" as quickly as possible, usually before the announcement came.

In this moment, no "at ease" was forthcoming, as was no oral communication from either of the senior officers. Captain Stilton simply stood, looking at the three men, frowning. As the silence was climbing their backs like some sadistic medieval torture for the three men, Red, as Bert's senior petty officer, was compelled to break the silence. "Captain, I think this can all be explained," he hopefully entreated.

"I want you, Petty Officer Cook, to shut your pie-hole and leave. The same with you, Chief Boggs."

Both looked at one another with horror. It was tradition for the "accused" enlisted man to be accompanied by his senior enlisted petty officers, and it was also tradition for the captain to at least maintain some semblance of decorum and due process. That was apparently not happening in this matter, and as the two left the captain's stateroom, they took with them a look of angst that communicated to Bert this was not going to go well.

"Have a seat, Seaman Bertram," the captain stated with a continuing look of gravity on his face. "I'm looking at a whole slew of charges, and I'm trying to decide whether to put you in the brig and then send you to court-martial when we get back to Pearl or whether to deal with this myself." To Bert's knowledge, a small ship like the *Peckham* had no brig, but he wasn't going to argue the point.

"You could be looking at jail time, a dishonorable discharge, and a tough future for yourself if I go that way," stated the CO. "On the other hand, if we go the Captain's Mast way, I can bust you to E-1, dock your pay, confine you to ship for the rest of your enlistment, and generally make your life miserable right here on my own ship."

Neither sounded like a good choice to Bert, but he preferred not to go to prison and definitely didn't want a dishonorable discharge. "There is a third option, however, that I want to offer you, and then I'll let you make the choice which way to go."

A third option? How on earth could there be a third option? And why on God's green little planet would the captain allow me to choose my own fate? Bert sensed an infinitesimal glimmer of hope for a moment, while at the same time trying to convince himself that being keel-hauled or being made to walk the plank into shark-infested waters was no longer being used as a punishment in the navy.

"As you know, Seaman Bertram, we have been putting together a landing force deployment team at the request of our chief of naval operations, and each team is required to be all-volunteer. We have tried everything to encourage a radioman to volunteer for the radio operator position on the LFDT but without success. Without a radioman, we'll have no team, and this will be very bad for LT Commander Hawthorne and me, as we won't be able to provide a team as requested. May I ask why you were reluctant to volunteer for this position?"

Reluctant was far from where Bert's sense of volunteerism landed on this matter. *Loath* would have been a much better word. During boot camp, Bert had volunteered for several jobs that turned out to be nightmares, and it wasn't until Wonder lectured Bert after volunteering for a work party that the acronym NAVY stood for "Never Again Volunteer Yourself." The mere idea of spending weeks in the mud in some sort of special operations training or in the jungle in some kind of military warfare training or in any of the other macho body builder, football star required trainings sounded like the worst possible thing that anyone could undergo. No, Bert was absolutely averse to even considering that notion. Of course, he did not voice his opposition quite so enthusiastically in this venue, considering the circumstances. "I guess I never really gave it much thought," was all Bert could squeak out to the captain.

"Well, today, Seaman Bertram, you just put your bet on red 21, and it has paid off. I am willing to discharge all charges against you and will leave your modest service record intact. We'll just forget about your lapses in judgment the other night on the quarterdeck, provided, in the next fifteen seconds, you officially volunteer to be the radioman on our landing force deployment team and also provided you graduate the absolutely stellar training that will be provided to you with this opportunity."

Bert looked at LTJG Hudson, whose face had drained of all blood and was doing his best to erase the look of absolute horror on his face. It was obvious to Bert that Rock was relishing the moment that maximum punishment was meted out to Bert. Bert looked back at Captain Stilton and smiled.

Well, there it was. Jail, dishonorable discharge, fines, being busted and confined, all would disappear, in exchange for eight weeks of living hell. It was almost as easy a choice as the one his father had presented to join the navy in the first place.

As Bert shook himself out of his reminiscences, he wondered, as he would several times in the future, whether he got the raw end of the deal. Now, this final bit of training was about to be completed, if he was able to find his way out of the jungle and to the landing zone in time to catch his helicopter. It was difficult not to criticize himself for protecting B.S.'s dentures, and even with all he would go through, in retrospect, he would have done it all over again.

13

A FREQUENT WIND

By March of 1975, it was clear that the North Vietnamese would soon occupy the entire country of Vietnam. The last of the prisoners of war had been returned two years prior, and now that it was apparent the North Vietnamese were executing a plan to conquer all of South Vietnam, it became a mad rush to evacuate the country. *Operation Frequent Wind*, the Pentagon's code name for the evacuation of South Vietnamese allies, the remaining State Department employees, and the last of the US servicemen had been in process for several months. The US government had identified more than 1,600,000 South Vietnamese officials and citizens who should and could be removed prior to the arrival of the PAVN, the North Vietnamese People's Army of Vietnam into Saigon. A massive number of transport planes had been gathered to fly out of Tan Son Nhut airport, the closest commercial airport to Saigon, to safety. The PAVN realized the strategic importance of this airport and bombed it into obliteration. This left only helicopters to transport as many people as possible. The defense attaché's headquarters was quickly chosen as an alternate base of operations, but when that became unworkable, the US embassy in Saigon was the next and final choice. Americans watched the nightly news to see crowds pleading with US Marines to let them in the gates of the embassy, coupled with scenes of helicopters taking off and landing atop the roof of the embassy. At sea, aircraft carriers were dumping helicopters and planes off their sides into the ocean to make way for more helicopters filled with the refugees. With the failure of the massive airlift, tens of thousands of South Vietnamese struggled to make their own way out of the country on chartered planes at first and when that option ended, boats of every size and shape, many of them filled with hundreds more people than they could hold. In the end, Operation Frequent Wind ferried a total of 1,373 Americans and just under 6,000 Vietnamese and other foreign nationals by helicopter. On April 30, 1975, the US embassy was under the control of the PAVN, and US involvement in Vietnam officially ended, with more than a million and a half South Vietnamese supporters still in the country. The government officially declared the Vietnam "Conflict" finished on May 15, 1975, and the US government's propaganda machine went into action, convincing the American public that the United States had no more involvement in Southeast Asia, including Cambodia. Because of government denials, a militarized CIA, and public weariness with anything happening in Indochina, the topic disappeared from media attention, and the US government intentionally focused the public on American's foremost enemy, the Soviet Union, and the Cold War.

Manny and Huck watched the messages arriving from CINC-PACFLT, their Pacific command, regarding Operation Frequent Wind and the evacuation of Saigon. Both knew that this meant they would soon be receiving orders to depart Squid Island. Manny gave the orders to begin disassembling the more permanent weapons and to proceed with the process of packing up and shipping out, knowing that it was just a matter of weeks before the order would come to make tracks. As they had been there more than eight months, this was no small task and needed to be well organized.

As Manny, Huck, and Coyote finished their impromptu staff meeting to organize the process of extraction, the radio came to life with the sound of their eastern sentry announcing that he had spotted two Khmer Rouge gunboats poking around off the island's coastline. This was the first time they had seen any sign of the Cambodians in their entire tenure on Squid Island. This was *not* good news, and they crossed their fingers that the platoon had not been spotted. Manny and Huck jogged to the eastern sentry's location, and grabbing the binoculars, Manny felt the hair on the back of his neck stand tall. About a mile out to sea, he could clearly see the two gunboats, as another came alongside them. They were making no definitive advances toward Squid Island, but it was pretty clear that the days of volleyball and long afternoon naps was about to take a turn for the more dramatic.

The ambient light in the jungle gradually brightened, which brightened Bert's hope that he was heading in the right direction to meet the helicopter. He made his way in the direction he believed was somewhat close to where the helicopter would be waiting for him and the others who had been on their own final "exam" during the last three days. The dense jungle began thinning, which was a very good sign, as helicopters need open area to land. Bert was usually a very optimistic person, but the past three days had tried his optimism more than anything in his life. He felt that optimism gradually returning as his brain carried him back to his life on the *Bob E*. This reminded Bert of his transit home from deployment following the denture debacle.

14

WALKING THE GREEN LINE

With the USS *Peckham* steaming toward home and Bert out of immediate hot water, the leisurely cruise time back to Pearl Harbor was an opportunity for a much-needed breather for most of the crew, as well as an opportunity for most of the crew to give their livers a repose. Daily work routines aside, Bert was in the process of completing a mountain of paperwork for his next "adventure," and within a day, he and the other fourteen sailors who had actually volunteered for the LFDT had already had several meetings. The first meeting was to introduce everyone who would be on the team and the team's leadership. The LFDT had already received a nickname from the crew: *the Ducks*. The nickname started with some of the crew suggesting that fifteen out-of-shape, completely untrained fleet sailors pretending to be a combat operations team were "ducks out of water." The name "Ducks" stuck like superglue to skin, and try as they might to change it, the name seemed to be one they would have to live with. The team preferred the pronounced acronym, LFDT. It was pronounced "Leff-Deet," which Bert did not consider to be much better. He figured that ducks out of water was apropos, considering the circumstances, and much better than the situation he feared the nickname might be describing "sitting ducks."

The team leader was the ship's weapons officer, or WEPO, LT Max Hoffelmeyer, a ruggedly handsome Naval Academy graduate, who looked a bit like Bert imagined the head of the Hitler Youth had looked. Hoffelmeyer was very tall and well-muscled and had a very short (not quite like Hitler but close) mustache, a shock of golden-blond hair, and the bluest eyes Bert had ever seen. That LT Hoffelmeyer had ended up in the fleet navy was a surprise, as it was obvious to Bert from his appearance that Hoffelmeyer was destined to head up torture for the CIA. Hoffelmeyer's unofficial nickname by the enlisted men who worked for him was "Lex," after Lex Luthor, Superman's nemesis. During the first meeting of the Ducks, the appropriateness of the nickname became obvious. LT Hoffelmeyer was enthusiastically taking the mantle of commander of the group and left no doubt that he was serious about the success of the LFDT.

"Gentlemen," LT Hoffelmeyer stated with intensity, "we have been given the most important assignment in the United States Navy."

Bert thought to himself there just might be a few more important jobs, like Navy SEAL, underwater demolitions, or surgeon, but he wasn't about to argue the point.

"... and we are going to be the standard by which all others are judged," said Hoffelmeyer, as he paced back and forth among the men. Bert was wondering if Hoffelmeyer secretly kept a swagger stick and halfway expected it to come out at any point.

"As such, I expect complete discipline, focus, and your most extreme effort in completing training, so that we can be prepared to engage in any and all missions the navy calls upon us to undertake."

Wow, thought Bert, *this guy is completely over the top*. Bert's initial curiosity with the demeanor of LT Hoffelmeyer was suddenly transformed to horror as he introduced his second in command, Lieutenant Junior Grade Owen Hudson, a.k.a. Rock. *Oh crap*, thought Bert as he stood in stunned silence at the sight of his worst nightmare. LTJG Hudson was now the ship's navigator, and Bert had spent an inordinate amount of time unsuccessfully avoiding him at all cost, and this was no different. Silently, Bert wondered what bad thing

LTJG Hudson had done to deserve this assignment. Bert couldn't help fretting about the combination of LT Hoffelmeyer and LTJG Hudson, Hoffelmeyer's miniature clone, and the hell he was about to enter.

Bert's attention began to wander to the other members of the team as LT Hoffelmeyer rambled into a speech that Bert found very reminiscent of the speech that Colonel Nickelson gave to his troops in the movie *Bridge on the River Kwai*. The enlisted men on the team were from various divisions of the ship. The hospital corpsman, HC1 "Doc" Doonan was well-known on the ship, both as the senior corpsman and the ship's most evangelistic Christian. Every corpsman in the navy is nicknamed "Doc," which can be quite confusing when there are several corpsmen in one place. Bert was not sure what they did to distinguish themselves when they gathered in classes or in hospitals together. Doc Doonan was never seen without a handful of Bible tracts, which he passed out like a heroin dealer giving sample drugs to schoolyard children. Bert thought it would have been a bit difficult doing his job on deployment, diagnosing and treating so many cases of crabs, scabies, and clap, but along with a penicillin shot, a VD patient was certain to receive a Bible tract ... or ten.

Most of the other team members were sailors whom Bert would have expected to be volunteers for the Ducks. Most were gunner's mates, with the exceptions of Petty Officer Third Class Scott "Scooter" Limcek and Seaman Al Todeski. Bert liked Scooter and had shared beers with him on several occasions. Scooter was, by Bert's assessment, a very easygoing and peaceful guy, who got along with pretty much everyone on the ship. His job on the ship was as a supply clerk, helping with payroll, supplies, and such, and he seemed a very unlikely kind of guy to volunteer for the Ducks. "I guess I'm just bored with paper," Scooter said when Bert asked about his motivations. "I like camping and hiking, so I thought it would just be nice to get outside for a change." Scooter was from Seattle, Washington, and while Bert had never been there, his image of the people in the Northwest was as either "tree huggers" or lumberjacks, and all he knew about the area was that it rained a lot there, something that was a rare occurrence in New Mexico. Scooter's favorite joke about Washington was to reply to the inevitable commentary from someone outside of the state that it rained all the time there, "No, it only rained twice last week, once for three days and once for four." Scooter seemed to Bert more like a tree-hugging liberal environmentalist and not so much a lumberjack. Bert had never seen anyone quite as mellow as Scooter, and try as he might, he just couldn't imagine Scooter with a rifle in his hands shooting at the enemy, much less shooting anything else.

Rounding out the team was Seaman Al "Toad" Todeski, a jovial and very hefty radar operator. Once again, Toad seemed to Bert to be an unlikely candidate for the team, as all Bert had ever seen him do was drink beer and eat the most amazing array of junk food. His junk food habits were renowned on the ship, and he ultimately had been rationed by his division officer, as Toad was getting too large to fit through door hatches and into his seat at the radar scope. Toad's division officer had him on a strict diet and was attempting to slim him down with physical exercise. Reluctantly, Toad had also "volunteered" for the team in exchange for a lifting of his junk food ban at the ship's store.

"So, let's review the schedule for training," Hoffelmeyer continued, which brought Bert's attention back to the meeting. "We pull into port on May 5. You have one week to see and say goodbye to your families before boarding a transport plane headed for Camp Pendleton for a two-week, shortened version of Marine Combat Training, just to get you warmed up. The marines have quickly put together a special course for us, just like all our training. You will train and learn together, outside of the military members who enrolled in the actual courses. Each course has been abbreviated so that we can complete our entire LFDT training in eight weeks. Two of you will be chosen to also attend Marine Corps Scout Sniper Training, or at least a shortened version of that school. Following MCT, you'll head to the Naval Special Warfare School in Coronado. Yes, team, you'll be trained by Navy SEAL instructors with emphasis on physical training, basic underwater demolitions, land combat training, underwater combat training, and other important skills, just like you were training to be a SEAL, only you'll once again have a condensed course of three weeks. Now, LTJG Hudson and I won't be training with you. They have set up a separate officer's course with a slightly different skill set, so we'll meet you back at the *Peckham* after training." This seemed a bit counterintuitive to the enlisted members, since, if they were going to be called on a mission, they would all have to work together. *Oh well, that's the navy*, was the mind balloon above each sailor's head.

Bert had heard that normally, Navy SEAL training Phase I was twenty-four weeks and was only about a third of the entire SEAL training. He was trying to imagine how they could possibly learn anything of value in three weeks.

"Finally," LT Hoffelmeyer declared, "we'll head off to Camp Lejeune to the Second Marine Reconnaissance division, to be trained in marine special operations. Once again, this will be a condensed, two-week course. From there, you'll be flown to Subic Bay for Jungle Survival School and to SERE: Survival, Evasion, Resistance, and Escape Compound, a comprehensive training in POW survival for five days. As I mentioned, two of you who have shooting expertise will be chosen to attend Marine Corps Scout Sniper Training at the new Marine Corps Air Station at Kaneohe Bay. I'm expecting that my gunner's mates on the team will have no problem qualifying for that. If all goes well, you'll go through a formal graduation ceremony with the commander of the Pacific Fleet on July 7, and you'll be back with the ship on July 8."

As the team was leaving the briefing, LTJG Hudson stepped over and leaned his face uncomfortably close to Bert's ear. "Fuck this up, Bertram," barked Rock, "and you will see my wrath." As he turned and left the room, he pointed at Bert and said, "That I promise."

Well, at least he's predictable, thought Bert.

"Holy shit," whispered Toad to Bert. "I'm gonna fuckin' die." Bert didn't answer, as he was mulling over asking the captain just to go ahead and send him to court-martial.

The remaining couple of weeks sailing back to Pearl Harbor were a joy to experience for Bert—great weather, lots of outdoor time, and since he had been pulled for the Ducks and was expected to begin study, he was not required to stand watches. Thanks to Lucky, Bert had his new spare printer, which made teletype repair much more leisurely. This all gave Bert the time to listen to long, droning, boring team lectures "performed" by LT Hoffelmeyer. The truth was, there wasn't a lot for Hoffelmeyer to say, as nobody had much of an idea what to expect. They were the first guinea pigs for this grand experiment, and other than receiving some cool training uniforms that made them look like badass marines, they didn't have much to do. That allowed Bert to relax, sleep in, take naps, read, and sunbathe, which helped to assuage his ever-increasing anxiety about the training, just a bit.

One afternoon, the captain stopped the ship in calm waters and gave the crew "swim call." The gunner's mates would stand shark watch with rifles, and for an hour or so, the crew was permitted to dive off the ship and swim in the water. It was an unusual treat, as ships are usually on a tight schedule, but it was greatly appreciated by all who took advantage of the opportunity. Grown sailors became little boys again, doing flips and dives from the upper decks of the *Peckham*, splashing and swimming in the deep blue sea.

The *Bob E.* returned to port on schedule, and as was tradition, all the sailors were in their dress whites, standing at the railings. Families were permitted on the pier and were reunited with their loved ones. While Bert had no family in Pearl Harbor, it was no less a heartwarming experience to watch the reunions of his shipmates with their families.

As promised, one week later, the entire LFDT team was dressed in their training uniforms, packed, and on the tarmac at Hickam Air Force Base, boarding an Air Force C-130. The next morning, the team drove through the gates of US Marine Corps Base, Camp Pendleton, a sprawling, 125,000-acre facility designed primarily for training. The sailors were met by Sergeant Jake Wallings, Company E MCT training instructor, and his assistants. Sergeant Wallings, used to training young marines fresh out of boot camp, initially approached the team just as he would have his marines. "Okay, girls, off the van and get in formation!" Wallings shouted. Since this wasn't boot camp, and his students weren't marines, he was a bit unsure how to deal with them. His supervisor had told him to treat them just as he would marines. "LFDT sailors, form up!" he shouted again.

The sailors were casually getting out of the van, and it appeared to Sgt. Wallings that they had no idea how to "form up." He was correct in this observation. All the sailors had been to boot camp at some point, learned to march with a rifle, and learned how to form up, but following boot camp, forming up was a much more casual affair than Sgt. Wallings was used to. Trying not to become too frustrated, he repeated the order once more and then started explaining what forming up meant. It took some doing, but eventually, the sailors were somewhat close to a military formation.

"I'm Sergeant Wallings, and I'll be your primary instructor for the nine, er, two-week course." When Wallings was informed that he was going to have to take a group of completely untrained sailors through a rigorous marine combat course in two weeks, he immediately realized the unfeasibility of this challenge, but, as a good marine, he and the staff put together a course that they could use to at least casually paint some marine combat skills on the team.

"Let me start by informing you of the purpose of this training to the Marine Corps. One of our mantras is 'every marine a rifleman.' What this means is that learning basic combat skills is mandatory for every single marine regardless of what their MOS will be. It doesn't matter whether a marine is a driver, a supply geek, or a cook, every marine is first and foremost a rifleman.

"This course is usually nine weeks, and I've been informed that you all have had about nine minutes of weapons training, so getting you anywhere close to proficient is going to be a challenge for you rust pickers. Nevertheless, you will be introduced to weapons skills, including the handling and firing of the M16, the M203 grenade launcher attached to the M16 with forty-millimeter grenades, the M240 machine gun, and the M1911 Colt forty-five pistol. You will be expected to qualify at the range with both the M16 and the M1911.

Additionally, you will be instructed on convoy operations, combat hunter skills, offensive/defensive fundamentals, tactical communications and land navigation. Combat conditioning hikes, fitness runs, and Marine Corps martial arts sustainment will be on the agenda while attending this course. Even though we both know you are not marines, it is my intention to treat you just as I do the marines I train. I will require you to be tough, learn quickly, and respond to orders unquestioningly. I expect you to do your very best, um, considering the circumstances. Our first step will be to get you settled into the barracks and issue you PT and training gear; then we'll start with physical training this afternoon. Any of you *rust pickers* have a question?"

Todeski raised his hand and said, "Yes, Sergeant, can you tell me when lunch is, and any chance of catching a little nap before we go PT ourselves?"

Sergeant Wallings stared at the rotund sailor and failing to keep a look of spite and incredulity off his face, suspected that, including three tours in Vietnam, he was now in for the biggest challenge of his career.

Sergeant Wallings's suspicions were confirmed and reinforced almost immediately. Fifteen sailors were to actively participate in condensing nine weeks of training into two weeks, and perhaps five of these men were in decent physical shape, only a few had ever had experience with firearms, and none had any combat training. *Fat chance*, thought Wallings. The team mustered in thirty minutes for their first physical training session, and Wallings's observation was that it was a bit like rehabilitating the bodies of astronauts who had been in space for six months. He was completely unable to fathom how these people even walked to the mess hall for food without dropping dead from exhaustion. Granted, most were giving it a try, but it became evident that MCT physical training would put them in traction. So, Wallings and his assistants dumbed-down PT on the fly, and their first foray was ten push-ups, ten pull-ups—which most were unable to do—fifty sit-ups, and a half-mile jog or at least a run-walk. Sergeant Wallings mentally noted that it was a bit like teaching first grade PE.

For the first few days, Wallings tried the Marine Corps way, rousting the sailors at 0500 for PT and attempting to instill any form of discipline in the team, all with little or no success. Most were an embarrassment on the firing ranges, with several near misses of buildings, marines, and themselves, and half of his class dozed-off during classroom instruction. Basic land navigation was a disaster, and he lost one of the sailors who was wandering on the navigation course until midnight one night, requiring the recruitment of some K-9 handlers to use dogs to find him.

"This is an impossible mission," Wallings complained to his first sergeant. "They don't listen, they have no discipline, they are out of shape, they have little to no skills of any kind. Whatever mission they are being trained for is going to fail miserably."

"Here's the deal, Jake," said the first sergeant. "We are under orders to do the best we can. Command is watching us very closely, so we must do our best to put on a good show. Take good notes each day, and we'll report it on to command. I see no problem in putting the best spin on the training. Try to find some bright spots to put in your nightly reports. In the meantime, do the best you can, but don't stress over it. Just get them through the two weeks so we can pass them off to someone else."

It was a very long two weeks for both Sergeant Wallings and the Ducks. Most had never exercised the way they were now, even in navy boot camp, even considering Wallings stepping-down the level of training to what he considered an eight-year-old soccer team could handle. For Bert, the physical training was hard, but it was good to feel some strength and endurance coming back. As his joy in high school was shooting his twenty-two, he thoroughly enjoyed the weapons training. Navy vessels don't usually carry M16s or any sort of automatic weapons, as automatic weapons inside the equivalent to a tin-can could be disastrous. Bert's first experience on the range with M16s made him realize that he was just shooting a fancy, badass twenty-two. His first attempt at qualifying at the range yielded him a score of 175, which qualified him for expert marksman and the navy marksman medal, even though he was shooting at the wrong target for his first five shots. In fact, he was pretty sure that he qualified Scooter, who was next to him, for the sharpshooter medal. He was especially proud that he shot better than the gunner's mates, who had all been given instruction and range time with these weapons in their gunner's mate training.

By the last few days of the two-week course, Sergeant Wallings was simply going through the motions. In fact, he had gone to the point of calling an instructor friend at the Naval Special Warfare Center to warn him of the assemblage of Gomers that were about to descend on whatever remedial-level course the SEALS had created.

The final night at MCT, the team was in a deep funk. They realized that they weren't marines and didn't have the physical capacity and skills necessary to serve as competent warriors, but it was difficult to have been the target of such condescension and disdainful patronization. They *were* trying. They knew they were in a difficult position, and they appreciated the difficult position that Sergeant Wallings was in, yet they were, in fact, feeling quite demoralized. They did not like to be considered a bunch of incompetent clowns, and it was tough to know that was exactly how they were viewed.

The team was hopeful that their next training experience at the Naval Special Warfare Center would prove to be a change for the better, since they would be trained by fellow sailors rather than marines. With a halfhearted goodbye from Sergeant Wallings, the Ducks boarded a van for the short ride from Camp Pendleton to the Naval Special Warfare Center in Coronado, California. NSWC Coronado is where the US Navy's and perhaps the world's most proficient special forces troops, the SEALS, are born, raised, and trained. Just getting into SEAL training is a monumental task that involves swimming laps with backpacks of bricks on, mental exams, physical endurance tests, and much more. Very few who attempt to join are successful at gaining entrance to the elite training. Navy SEAL training is considered the most rigorous in the world, and to the navy, it is called BUD/S Training (Basic Underwater Demolitions/SEAL).

For aspiring Navy SEALs, the initial training is twenty-four weeks of pure challenge. And challenge is an understatement. The training curriculum begins at Naval Special Warfare Preparatory School in Great Lakes, Illinois. There, aspiring SEALs are given a crash course in the physical standards required to even attempt to become a SEAL.

The SEAL candidate's official training starts with an initial physical screening test and ends with an even more demanding physical screening test, one that includes a timed four-mile run and a timed 1,000-meter swim. The goal is to increase the SEAL candidates' physical readiness between the two tests so that they are ready to move on to BUDS/S training. Those unable to pass the final test, which are the majority, are removed from the SEAL training pipeline and sent back to the fleet navy. Those candidates who are successful in completing this portion move on to the BUD/S twenty-four-week training, which includes much more indoctrination and physical conditioning. To the SEALs, that means doing things like running miles on the beach carrying telephone poles, four-mile timed runs in boots and packs, and two-mile swims. The first two weeks of basic conditioning prepare candidates for the third week, also known as "Hell Week." During Hell Week, candidates participate in five and a half days of continuous training. Each candidate sleeps (at most) four hours during the entire week, runs more than 225 miles, and undergoes incredibly rigorous physical training for more than twenty hours per day. The remaining four weeks involve plenty of "book" learning, including various methods of conducting underwater surveys and making underwater maps. It is an understatement to say that very few candidates move past Hell Week, and all the candidates can quit at any time. After Hell Week comes combat diving training, then land warfare training, and in the final five weeks, the candidates are taken offshore about sixty miles, where they practice all the skills learned in all three phases. Many students view this as one of the hardest parts of training, as training is conducted seven days a week, with only a couple of hours of sleep each night, while at the same time handling live explosives and ammunition. Interaction with instructors is continuous, and punishments from those instructors are at their harshest levels of the entire course. By the end of the third phase, candidates must complete a timed two-mile ocean swim with fins in seventy-five minutes, a four-mile timed run with boots in thirty minutes, and a fourteen-mile run in full combat gear.

By the time the Ducks arrived in Coronado, news of their amazing incompetence coupled with the futility of successful training had spread throughout the instructors at the center, and unfortunately for the team, the awaiting instructors assumed attitudes toward the training that would, at best, be called, "I don't give a fuck. Let's get them through these three weeks and send them on." This resulted in minimal physical training (enough to satisfy superiors), minimal weapons training, and highly contracted time in the pools, on the inflatables, and in the field. Despite the hopes the Ducks had that this time they would be treated as "real" students, it quickly became three weeks that they had to occupy NSWC training camp, get it done, and then depart, and so both the team and the instructors conspired to make that as easy a process as possible.

Surprisingly, Bert was a bit disappointed with the lack of enthusiasm the instructors showed during training. He wasn't disappointed at the lack of abuse, but even with the survey of the basics of the job of a Navy SEAL, Bert gained great appreciation for those who successfully graduated. The good side of the lackadaisical attitude of the instructors was that it made the training feel more like Boy Scout summer camp, only with real combat weapons, camping out, underwater gear, and getting to blow stuff up.

The unenthusiastic SEAL instructors bade adieu to the Ducks (by this time, *everyone* called them the Ducks), breathed a sigh of relief at their departure, and went back to giving hell to *real* SEAL candidates but not before passing on the word to the instructors at the Marine Reconnaissance Battalion that they should treat the Gomers as though they were severely physically and mentally impaired men and to avoid wasting their time putting any effort into the Ducks.

As the somewhat demoralized group arrived and were greeted by instructors from Force Reconnaissance, they entered the van with the lowest expectations of any of the classes, as they were back with the marines. During the van ride from Albert J. Ellis Airport to Marine Base Camp Lejeune, North Carolina, Gunnery Sergeant Thomas "Tank" McGee introduced them to the base and went over the crux of their training. Sergeant McGee explained to the Ducks that the marines historically had never had a separate special forces designation, instead relying upon good marine training for all. During Vietnam, Marine commanders realized that there were skills that their rifle companies just didn't possess, and as such, the corps put concerted effort into teaching advanced skills to qualified marines and created "Marine Reconnaissance Units." The Force Recon platoons operated farther inland than their regular marine counterparts, penetrating deeper into enemy territory from what was traditionally the operating area for marines, which had been the coastal areas. Force Recon operated at such great distances that they were beyond the reach of the support that other marines relied on, which was usually artillery and the big guns from naval ships. Consequently, for Force Recon, silence and stealth were their critical weapons. Force Recon existed to gain information through deep reconnaissance, direct action, and the control of supporting arms to convey military intelligence beyond the means of a commander's area of influence in the battlefield. Force Recon operated independently in combined amphibious and ground operations to support marine operations, and because of this, a prevailing philosophy in Force Recon was that *if a single round is fired, the mission is deemed to have failed.* That is not to say that Force Recon was not trained in special operations missions, and throughout the Vietnam conflict, they were called upon numerous times for such operations. Force Recon was never a part of the US Special Operations Command, mostly because their missions were subtly different from those of other Special Operations Forces units. In official marine statements, Force Recon was "Specialized in all tactical areas of warfare. Force Recon will train with other Special Operations forces, such as US Navy SEALs, US Army Special Forces, and US Air Force Pararescue, in order to master all skill sets. The Marine Corps has seen fit to train versatile specialists rather than specialists in individual areas of combat."

The team saw Gunny McGee make a very serious face as he turned from the front passenger seat of the van back to talk to them. "Sailors, I have spoken with your instructors both at MCT and at BUD/S training, and, guys, quite frankly, I have to be honest with you, they didn't have much good to say. I understand that you haven't been training mentally or physically the way that others are trained in their respective schools, and I was given the advice to coddle you, give you a pleasant two weeks, and to have little or no expectations of any sort of competence from any of you.

"But," continued Gunny, "I guess eighteen years in the Marine Corps and particularly the last eleven years in Recon has taught me something a bit different. What I and my staff are going to do is to teach you how to observe, how to move with stealth, how to hide yourself from the enemy, and how to be opportunistic in what you observe.

"I know you've been taught to shoot various weapons, and you're not in the best of shape physically, and you all come from a pretty sedentary life aboard ship. I'm going to work with that. Even though many of my counterparts consider this entire LFDT idea to be a deeply flawed concept by ivory tower officers with stars on their collars who have no concept of how we work in the real world and consequently deserving of the minimum attention in order to accomplish our assigned mission, I've decided to take a slightly different approach. I'm going to assume that, God forbid, you all might be called upon to engage in a real-world mission at some point in the future. If you are, I don't want anything I have done during my time with you to jeopardize your lives or the lives of others, if I can at all prevent that. My two goals are to teach you enough skills to at least help you to come back alive and perhaps, with the grace of God, make a mission successful. If we accomplish anything more in our time together, so be it. But I want you to know that you all may just be called upon to do something in the future that you aren't quite prepared for. My job is to give you some skills to think it through and make good tactical decisions in a place where mayhem is going on all around you. I know we only have two weeks, so I'm going to try to teach you the most important things you should know if you're ever called out."

Bert looked around at the others and observed that this was the first time they had been spoken to with any kind of respect since the beginning of training, and as he watched the others, each was riveted to the words of Gunny. It felt like, for the first time since training had begun, they were starting to get the fact that they weren't just "playing army" and that the skills that these professionals were trying to impart might just, one day, be necessary to employ.

The next two weeks were completely fascinating to Bert. They learned such foreign concepts as how to set a perimeter to protect a platoon; how to hide in plain sight; how to set snares, traps, and trip-wires; how to use claymore landmines effectively; and how to observe the enemy without being seen, as well as camouflage techniques and advanced land navigation. Bert could easily see that it would take far more than two weeks to become proficient at this, but he and the other Ducks walked away with a huge appreciation for the "art" of warfare and how effective intelligence gathering and independent thinking without the benefit of outside guidance might someday for them be critical to survival.

Following the training at Camp Lejeune, the Ducks were transported to Naval Jungle Survival School in Subic Bay. This trip to Subic would not include any visits to Olongapo. They would be training at the navy's jungle survival school, which was a portion of the huge naval base in Subic Bay. All Navy pilots and flight crews were required to attend as a matter of course. During Vietnam, it became evident that jungles tended to be magnets for downed aircraft and that without adequate skills, an aviator might survive being shot down only to die in a peril-filled jungle. The classroom portion of the course was fascinating to Bert, and the instructors taught excellent skills, such as navigation and hunting. Their first experience in an actual jungle took place during day two. They were all loaded into a van in the hills above the bay and stopped on a dirt road surrounded by thick trees and plants. The team was taken fifteen feet into the jungle and told simply to walk out. Thirty minutes later, they were not even close to the road. Bert was amazed that the jungle should be so close to a road, yet he immediately became as disoriented as he would have in a thick fog bank. It was a frightening dose of reality that improved everyone's attention on the instruction over the next few days.

The final exam of jungle survival school was to be helicoptered into the jungle, alone, and given thirty-six hours to travel to a designated pickup location. Each trainee was given a survival knife, five matches, three feet of fishing line, a compass, and a quart of water.

As Bert thought about this long, winding road that had brought him to this particular place, he was just a bit proud of himself and the others on his team. No, they weren't competent warriors. But they had gained some skills along the way that most likely would never be used. If nothing else, it would give him good stories to tell his grandchildren someday.

The jungle was clearing, and despite his minimal land navigation skills, Bert was less than a football field away from the landing zone. With a whoop and a jump, he kicked himself into high gear. He was at the LZ with two hours to spare on day three, and for the first time in the last month, he felt like he had accomplished the greatest victory of his life.

Upon finishing jungle survival school, the team went on the SERE (Survival, Evasion, Resistance, and Escape) school in which the air force had created a mock Vietnamese prison camp. They spent three days in training there.

The day of completion of SERE school, Bert was informed that he and Scooter had been chosen to go to Marine Scout Sniper Training, much to Bert's surprise and much to the chagrin of the gunner's mates on the team who were sure they would be selected. The basic course for the Third Marine Division was given in Kaneohe Bay on Oahu, so the entire team was flown back to Hawaii. Those who were not selected met the ship in Pearl Harbor, and Bert and Scooter were driven to Kaneohe Bay for Marine Scout Sniper School, or at least the Reader's Digest condensed version of the school.

During orientation, Bert and Scooter met Gunnery Sgt. Hammond "Ham" Dinsmore. "The Marine Corps has the best sniper program in the world," said Gunny Dinsmore, who was the staff noncommissioned officer in charge of the Scout Sniper School. "A sniper needs to be trained as best as possible because they must be combat ready at all times," he explained.

"Due to the nature of the sniper's mission, they must be trained mentally and physically to operate independently in front of their teams on the battlefield. This school goes further in depth than what regular marine units teach about basic marksmanship, weapons, camouflage, and reconnaissance techniques," said Dinsmore. "We train army, air force, and Navy SEALs at our school. So, we're the best of the best. Of course, this is going to be an abbreviated course for you two, but the good thing is, you two get private tutoring from me for this time."

The Scout Sniper course is broken down into three phases. The first involves land navigation and marksmanship. During this phase, trainees fire sniper ammunition on long-distance and unknown-distance qualification courses. The second phase covers stalking techniques, field skills, and "call for fire" rehearsals. The last encompasses everything from communication to surveillance performance. Gunny Hammond broke down the job of the sniper in a way Bert could understand. Bert came to learn that most people think of snipers as sneaky people who just randomly shoot people. In actuality, that's not even close to the truth. Marksmanship makes up only about 10 percent of being a sniper. Gunny Dinsmore was clear in this instruction, saying, "Frankly, patience and stealth are the two most important qualities of being a sniper." Gunny felt that pretty much anyone could be taught to shoot proficiently, but very few can survive the patience required to fire on the right target at the right time, in order to best support the mission. Bert learned that snipers could lie dormant for many hours and even days before pulling the trigger.

The Marine Scout Sniper School was great fun for Bert, and Gunny Dinsmore was funny, a kind teacher, and the most "Zen" human being he had ever met. It made sense to Bert, when he thought about it, that when 90 percent of your job is to sit and wait and wait and wait, you would need to have the skills of a Buddhist monk to be successful. Bert was oriented to the M21 sniper rifle. The army had used the XM21, which was a bolt-action hunting rifle with a super-scope. It had been introduced to the military in the second half of 1969 and was either loved or hated, depending upon with whom one spoke. An improved version now designated the M21 was in the process of being introduced to the military and was what potential scout snipers were being trained on. Unlike the single-cartridge rifles of early Vietnam, the M21 used a twenty-round box magazine. Already, there had been quite a bit of criticism of the rifle, and field snipers were reporting that its additional sophistication also made it highly susceptible to malfunctions. Many of the traditional snipers preferred the older rifles.

On the day of graduation, Bert and Scooter were both presented with M21s to use on the team, which were going to be shipped separately. Along with the new rifles and ammo, Bert and Scooter received a message from Gunny Dinsmore that the *Peckham* was leaving in three days for the West Pacific. This was far ahead of the proposed deployment schedule of October. Apparently, the USS *Holt*, which was supposed to be leaving on deployment had encountered a significant combat mission with a merchant ship, the SS *Mayaguez*, and a ship was needed to replace the USS *Holt*. Naturally, Captain Stilton had volunteered the *Bob E.*, so off they were, going on deployment much sooner than expected.

The *Bob E.* was off the coast of Oahu doing some final tweaking of its engineering, so Bert and Scooter were sent to Ford Island, where the ship would meet them. It was time for celebration, and Bert really liked the EM club on Ford Island, so Bert and Scooter headed there to wait for the *Peckham* to arrive. As they entered the club, they saw Toad at the bar. "What are you doing here, Toad?" asked Bert. "Aren't you supposed to be on the ship?"

"Got lucky and the chief left me here to hit the naval supply store for stuff for our division for the deployment," said Toad. "Let me buy you a beer. We really haven't had the chance to celebrate finishing LFDT training!"

"Yep, and good riddance," said Scooter. "With Nam officially done, I think we can put those skills on the shelf and go back to life as we know it!"

The three had a great time talking about the training, and, of course, Toad was very interested in learning about scout sniper school. There was great braggadocio as their self-estimation of their combat skills improved with each beer. They had a great time swapping stories and drinking far too much. They left the EM club and began walking back to the pier where the *Bob E.* was docked. The trip required a walk around Ford Island Airfield, or perhaps a bit of a stagger around the field. As they were walking past the airfield, Bert noticed a bright orange windsock flying behind the ten-foot fence with razor wire on top. Using all the judgment skills that a twenty-year-old drunk sailor can muster, Bert stopped and looking at the windsock, said, "I've got a great idea."

Toad, knowing the trouble Bert had been in that had precipitated his volunteering for the team, looked at him with great trepidation and anxiety as Bert revealed his plan. "Since we are now LFDT, let's use our new skills, infiltrate the airfield, and cut down the windsock!"

"Brilliant idea, Bert!" Scooter said with great enthusiasm.

"I think that idea stinks," said Toad.

"Great, then it's settled," pronounced Bert, and they proceeded to go on their first mission as LFDT. The new warriors, using as much stealth as three significantly intoxicated men can managed to breach the airfield perimeter and crawl on their hands and knees across the field, ducking when the airport lights flashed their way, rolling, tumbling, and acting just like what they thought the SEALS would do in this situation, although slightly louder and significantly less stealthy. They made it to the windsock pole without being spotted and plotted their strategy. From a hundred yards away, the pole looked quite a bit shorter than it did now. The pole had to be a good thirty feet high. Nevertheless, they decided one of them needed to climb the pole and cut it down. Toad was completely out, so Scooter volunteered for the most dangerous disposition. As he started climbing, he said, "Oh, shit, there's grease on this pole!" so with Toad standing on the bottom, pushing Bert onto his shoulders, who in turn pushed Scooter on top of his own, Scooter proceeded to climb the pole. Fortunately, at about twelve feet, the grease stopped. Scooter managed to shimmy the rest of the distance with his new combat knife in his mouth, just like he had seen pirates in movies carry their daggers. When he got to the top, he shouted down, "It looks like a brand-new windsock!"

"Great!" shouted Bert. "Now get cutting!"

Taking more time than perhaps the SEALS would have, Scooter hacked on the windsock until it came down and then lost his grip and came sliding down the pole like a fireman on nitro. He crashed into Bert, who crumbled onto Toad, and all three fell on their backs on the ground. Bert had the wind knocked out of him, and Toad's face had a cut from his temple to his cheek. Somehow, the three managed to get back to the ship, but before boarding, they threw the windsock into the lifeboat ledge; then, once aboard, they retrieved it.

The next morning was the first briefing of the new LFDT team aboard the ship. LTJG Hudson was not in the room at the beginning of the meeting, but once the meeting was underway, he came in using crutches. "LTJG Hudson sprained his ankle night before last after we returned from our schools," said LT Hoffelmeyer. "He'll be fine in a week or two."

The team spent a couple of hours debriefing and setting out the continuing drill schedule for the team. After the meeting, LT Hoffelmeyer asked Toad, Scooter, and Bert to stay behind. "Seaman Todeski," said LT Hoffelmeyer, "I can't help but notice that you have had an accident. Can you please explain?"

With chagrin, the three explained their exploits with the windsock, expecting reproof and perhaps even punishment. Instead, LT Hoffelmeyer shut the door, and, looking to his left and right as though someone were going to listen, smiled, and said, "Well, I'll be goddammed. I can't believe you three would do such a risky, immature act. I should be mad ... if it weren't for the fact that night before last, LTJG Hudson and I did exactly the same thing. That's why he has a bandage on his leg and crutches. Damn that pole was slick! I guess we both gained some skills during training, huh? Well, I have an idea for us to celebrate our first missions, and since you, Bert, are part of communications, it will take a conspiracy with your signalman chief."

Following LT Hoffelmeyer's instruction, each returned to his respective division to resume his "day job" on the ship.

The morning the ship left for deployment, the usual deployment ritual began on the *Bob E.* The sailors in their dress whites stood on the railing, families shouting and giving wave kisses to their loved ones, and as the ship passed the admiral's office on Ford Island, she was flying two bright-orange windsocks from the ends of the flag railings on the top of the ship, bidding farewell to Hawaii for the next four months.

Bert had high hopes for this deployment to end better than the last. He had a much better handle on his job in the radio shack and knew much better how to handle the temptations that came with liberty ashore. While this deployment would have similar stops to the last, he was excited that Bangkok, Thailand, had been added to the list. While Bert had been regaled with stories of the libidinous opportunities that Thailand offered, he was also looking forward to seeing another foreign country, eating the food, and sightseeing.

After a short stop on Midway Island for refueling, stretching legs, and watching the amazingly death-defying inelegant landings of the native population of gooney birds, they headed nonstop for Subic Bay. The sailors on the *Peckham* couldn't help but notice the paucity of ships in port, and they were informed that all of the marine transports and larger ships were heading back to Pearl Harbor or San Diego filled with repositioning marines. Without a thought of the strategic issues involved, it was a windfall for the *Peckham* sailors, as they practically had Olongapo to themselves.

Toward the end of July, the *Peckham* was in the Gulf of Thailand, heading for some well-deserved liberty in Bangkok. One afternoon, Bert was in his usual perch on the signal bridge, when the lookouts spotted something unusual. A mile or so ahead was a boat, which appeared to be fifty feet or so in length, dead in the water. Climbing all over the top deck was an almost solid mass of people, holding white sheets and screaming at the top of their lungs, hoping to get the *Peckham*'s attention. The captain called general quarters, which is the navy's version of a "red alert," which brought the ship's security team outside, armed with weapons. The gunner's mates trained the big 5 gun on the forecastle of the ship toward the suspicious boat.

As the *Peckham* approached the boat, it became obvious that there was little threat, while at the same time, a sight never before seen by a navy ship was unfolding ahead. It was indeed a boat, fifty-five feet in length, covered with such a mass of people that the boat was barely visible. The *Peckham* approached the boat, and the captain ordered full-stop about 150 feet from it. Even from that distance, they could smell a horrific stench. It was obvious that these people were in trouble.

Not having a protocol for such an encounter, the captain had the radiomen send a flash message to COMDESRON 33, the commodore in charge of the destroyer group that the *Peckham* was a member of, explaining the circumstances and asking for direction. A message came back to send a gig to the boat with armed sailors to see if anyone was able to speak English. The *Peckham* was in no way allowed to pull alongside and under no circumstances to allow anyone on the boat to board the *Peckham*. The gig brought back news that there were at least four hundred people on this small boat and that they were Vietnamese refugees, fleeing for their lives. Three days prior, they had been attacked by Malaysian pirates. Their younger women had been raped, the pirates had stolen what meager possessions they had, they had sabotaged the boat's engines, they had put oil in their drinking water supply, and they had cast the boat adrift.

Another message to the commodore yielded more instructions: Take food and water, first-aid supplies, charts, and the ship's doctor, along with engine mechanics over to the boat. Give the passengers the water and food and charts, see if the *Peckham*'s mechanics could repair the engines, but, once again, under no circumstances, were they to bring the occupants of the boat onboard. Fortunately, the physician for the destroyer squadron was onboard the *Peckham*, which is an unusual occurrence, so the ship's physician and the two hospital corpsmen went to the boat. They discovered a very grim situation on the boat. Three bodies of dehydrated passengers were found, several women were pregnant and close to delivery dates, most of the passengers were dehydrated, and many were close to sunstroke. The news from the engine room was equally dire. The engine was most likely beyond repair.

A message back to the commodore resulted in a short message saying that he was seeking guidance from his superiors. Bert and the other radiomen watched the messages going from the commodore, then from the commander of the Seventh Fleet to the CNO, and finally from the CNO to the office of the Joint Chiefs of Staff, who were consulting the president. Bert was ecstatic at being involved in something of such importance. In fact, because this was the first encounter with Vietnamese boat people and the US Navy, there were massive political implications. Under international law, if a navy ship brings a refugee onboard, he or she is granted automatic asylum, and the refugee becomes the responsibility of the US government. That becomes a political, not military issue. There was already a bit of political stress over the number of Vietnamese that the US was taking in following the end of the conflict two months prior.

It took almost a day, but finally permission was granted to bring the refugee boat alongside the *Peckham*, just to facilitate continued efforts to repair engines and provide food and water and for the medical staff to treat the sick, but, once again, under no conditions were they to bring a single person aboard. It would have been impossible for Bert to describe the overwhelming odor of death, fear, and human excrement. The Ducks were mobilized to provide guard over the passengers, and Bert felt incredibly uncomfortable brandishing his M16 and M1911 toward the wretched and obviously unthreatening group of refugees.

Between watching the refugees and radio watches, Bert and the other radiomen carried almost continuous messages to the captain from increasingly higher people on the chain of command and sending messages from the captain updating the situation back to the higher and higher echelons.

A full day after initially encountering the boat people, a final message came from a significant sender: *POTUS*. It was directly from the president! The message indicated that the president had made a decision as to how to respond. The engines were to be repaired; navigation, food, and water were to be provided; and the *Peckham* was *only* allowed to bring the refugees onboard in the event the refugee boat was to start sinking, in order to save lives. As the mechanics on the ship were certain it would be impossible to repair the engines, the captain stood on the bridge reading the message that Bert had brought to him. LT Hoffelmeyer and the XO were both next to the captain.

The captain gave both the news. "This comes from our commander in chief. We can only bring the refugees onboard if the boat is sinking." Captain Stilton walked out on the flying bridge at the side of the ship's bridge and stared at the boat, still carpeted with people from one end to the other. It took many long seconds as everyone on the bridge waited to hear from the captain. He walked back in and turned to LT Hoffelmeyer. "Lieutenant, I was given to understand that your LFDT was provided with phosphorous grenades. Is that correct?"

"Yes, sir, we have about a dozen of them," Hoffelmeyer responded.

The captain then turned to the executive officer. "XO, take another look at that boat. I think it's sinking. What do you think?"

The XO looked out, gave the captain a wry smile, and said, "Sir, I'm pretty sure you are correct."

The captain gave the orders to bring all of the refugees onto the ship immediately and set up a quarantine area on the helicopter deck, to clear out the helicopter hangar, and to put tents up. Once all the refugees were onboard, the boat was cast off, and the Ducks were given the opportunity to toss a couple of well-placed phosphorous grenades in the hold of the boat. As the boat was sinking, pictures were taken of the sinking boat to send back to command. The captain sent a message back that the boat had sunk, but all refugees were saved and brought aboard the *Peckham*.

The motley group of refugees came aboard. All of the sailors on the ship pitched in, donating clothes, extra blankets, and whatever comforts they could provide to the refugees. It was amazing to Bert that with a good shower and a clean set of clothes, the most pathetic group of human beings he had ever chanced to see turned into good-looking, happy, and striking human ones. Everyone, including the refugees, was aware that they had now been given sanctuary by the United States.

Unfortunately, the encounter was not over, as, once the refugees were safely onboard, they had to be transported somewhere. The *Peckham* was early into a deployment, and it was unfeasible for the *Peckham* to return to Pearl Harbor now. Besides, Pearl Harbor was a great distance, and while the weather was acceptable at the moment, the Gulf of Thailand and the South China Sea could be monstrously tempestuous, and a group of over four hundred people on a hangar deck could turn into a disaster. As the politicians in Washington worked to find a solution, they requested that the *Peckham* be allowed to moor in a safe harbor. No country was willing to allow this. It wasn't until the navy indicated that they would bring the lone remaining transport ship into the area to transfer the refugees that Thailand agreed to allow the *Peckham* to moor in the harbor of the resort area of Pattaya Beach for the sole purpose of transporting the refugees to the transport ship. Under no circumstances was the *Peckham* to allow any refugee to set foot in the country. As the *Peckham* was close to Pattaya Beach, a well-known Thai resort area, they set sail and arrived two days later in the harbor. While under-way, one of the expectant mothers had a child, and because the child was born on an American ship, he was an automatic citizen of the United States. *Robert Peckham Nguyen*, the new American citizen, was given a party by the sailors that evening.

As the refugees were transferred to the marine transport ship and it set sail for Pearl Harbor, the commodore decided to cancel the trip to Bangkok and instead give the sailors two days in Pattaya Beach, which was probably the best couple of days Bert had lived in his life. It was a liberty worth its weight in gold and included being chased by an elephant while on a motor scooter in the countryside and some well-deserved relaxation, much beer, and great food. As Bert was lying on the pristine white sandy beach during his liberty, he mused that the entire event had been his proudest moment, and from that time on, Bert's respect for Captain Stilton was unwavering.

15
A SHIT SANDWICH WITH SQUID

A s Manny fortified sentries, he speculated to himself that when Khmer Rouge commanders were informed of the possibility of US forces on Mūc Ong, they were delighted. From Manny's observations of the growing power of the Khmer Rouge, he thought that logically, from a political standpoint, the Khmer Rouge wanted to be considered a force to be dealt with, especially because of their conflict with the Vietnamese government. The Khmer genocide was in full swing, with hundreds of thousands being executed each month. Manny's realistic worry was the Khmer would attempt to humiliate the United States by targeting his marines.

The surveillance in the days following the marines' first observation of the Khmer swift boats confirmed that the Khmer knew Squid Island was occupied by hostiles. The marines did their best to increase the camouflage of the base operations, and they dismantled as much of the aerial signs of their presence as possible. Manny doubled the watches on both sides of the island, and everyone was back in marine uniform. While the anxiety in most of the other marines increased, for Huck, anxiety lessened. As a veteran marine, he was happy to see marine discipline return. He was working best when he was preparing for action, and he was busily working with his platoon to make any possible action successful. Manny was expecting help for extraction anytime, but they were now well into July, with no date promised.

On the third day following the sighting of the gunboats, a helicopter flew over without threat, and during the coming days, there was an increasing contingent of swift boats and flyovers. It became clear to Manny that the Cambodians were planning something, and nowhere in his brain was there a conclusion that involved a happy ending. He again sent messages to his company commanders indicating the urgency involved in leaving the island, and he was assured the command was making plans for extraction. The military and the president had just endured the *Mayaguez* incident a month prior, and no one from the president to the Joint Chiefs of Staff to the Marine Command was anxious to give the Khmer Rouge an opportunity to score another public relations coup over the United States. Unfortunately, massive redeployment of resources had been underway since the first week of June. As Saigon fell, every transport ship and marine division was busily moving to other strategic locations. Battle and deployment-weary marines and sailors were given liberal leave and extended "stand down" opportunities, and most of the warships had been moved to Yokosuka, Japan, or Pearl Harbor. A skeleton crew of marines were at Marine Base Okinawa, and the plain fact was that there simply were few marine options to extract them in the short-term. Nevertheless, the president, NSC, and Pentagon were busily looking for any way to recover Manny's platoon from Squid Island in order to avoid any further embarrassment and the public relations nightmare that a "not-really-ended Vietnam" would have among the American public.

When the message regarding the marines' plight on Mūc Ong reached the desk of CNO Ira Stephens, he faced the situation with both concern and interest. That afternoon was the first briefing of the Joint Chiefs at the Pentagon on the marine "situation" on Mūc Ong, and Ira prepared to attend the meeting with the primary question of how the navy could help. A quick review of the ships nearest the location showed a helicopter carrier, the USS *Iwo Jima*, LPH-2, which was in the Java Sea and over 1,300 miles from Mūc Ong, and the USS *Robert E. Peckham*, which was in the Gulf of Thailand, less than 450 miles from the island. The *Iwo Jima* was the perfect ship for this mission. A helicopter carrier and marine transport ship, she carried a full complement of twenty-five helicopters and, when at full strength, a crew of over six hundred. She could carry up to 2,000 marines. A relatively slow ship with a maximum steaming speed of twenty-two knots (about twenty-five miles per hour), she would take approximately three days to steam to the island, which just might be an acceptable time to recover the marines. Unfortunately, she only had onboard two marine platoons of thirty-five men each because of the re-deployment of marines Stateside. The *Iwo Jima* was currently steaming toward Okinawa, with a mission to load 1,600 marines aboard to transport to Hawaii to process for discharge. While the USS *Peckham* was also not the fastest ship on the seas, she would be able to reach the island in less than a day at full steam. Admiral Stephens had just read a report the day prior on the successful completion of the *Peckham*'s LFDT, with caveats that the instructors had deep concerns about the competence of the team's members for any combat mission. From Ira's perspective, however, this would most likely be a mission to extract the marines without the need for combat, and, frankly, at this point in the game, these were the only tools the navy had to offer short-term.

Ira had not, quite frankly, thought a great deal about his LFDT concept being used this quickly or in this way. He was still in the midst of putting his first five test teams through training, and the *Peckham*'s team had finished training just four weeks prior. Nevertheless, he asked his adjutant to put together a portfolio for the meeting of the Joint Chiefs that afternoon on the options the navy had available, including the LFDT on the *Peckham*, and to give orders to both the *Peckham* and the *Iwo Jima* to steam at full-speed to rendezvous nine miles southwest of Mūc Ong. He also sent a message to the

Peckham to ready their LFDT in the event they were needed, without any further explanation about the nature of the mission.

General Robert Hastings was in the process of retiring from the Marine Corps. He had served as commandant of the Marine Corps since 1972. The commandant of the Marine Corps, in addition to being the highest-ranking member of the corps, also sits on the Joint Chiefs of Staff. Hastings was "old school," having begun his service as a second lieutenant in 1943, during World War II. He served in Korea and Vietnam and was ready to begin his life of golf and great-grand-kids. At this final point in his career, Hastings had two primary tasks to accomplish: overseeing the withdrawal, redeployment, and discharge of marines from Indochina and directing the congression-ally mandated reduction in total marine troops to 194,000. Anyone and everyone who was even remotely close to a discharge date in the marines was being given early discharges, and in preparation for the reduction in forces, an inordinate number of marines were being transferred to California bases, Camp Pendleton being the priority. Any and all marine transport methods were being utilized to trans-port marines Stateside now, which left a huge gap in forces anywhere close to Southeast Asia—exactly Hastings's orders.

Rarely does the president of the United States attend meetings of the Joint Chiefs. The Joint Chiefs typically meet independently, and the chairman of the Joint Chiefs is tasked with, depending upon the administration and the current state of world affairs, meeting with the president on a weekly basis for briefings. The president ordi-narily attends such meetings only in moments of crisis, and then it is protocol for such meetings to take place in the White House Situa-tion Room. Because this was a regularly scheduled meeting of the chiefs and because the president was reticent for any information on this "situation" to be made public, he traveled to the Pentagon to attend their meeting that afternoon.

The meeting began with a rare lack of decorum. "What in the hell are US Marines doing in Cambodia?" the president bellowed. "I have been advised over and over by you, the CIA, and the NSC that everyone is out!"

"If I may, Mr. President," General Hastings answered, "these marines were in the process of being redeployed. The challenge was that we have had two significant military distractions in the last sixty days, the *Mayaguez* and the fall of Saigon. We just didn't have the resources, and up until a few weeks ago, the Khmer Rouge did not appear to have been aware the marines were there. We just didn't consider the marines to be under threat of discovery."

Admiral Chester Humphreys, the Chair of the Joint Chiefs of Staff, concurred, saying, "We do have several options for extracting the marines, Mr. President. Some are better than others, but I want you to be aware of those options."

Admiral Humphreys asked Admiral Stephens and General Hastings to present the options. Ira Stephens explained the order he had given for ships' movement to the area and provided information on the brand-new landing force deployment team on the USS *Peckham* and on the presence of the USS *Iwo Jima* as he presented the options. "The bottom line, Mr. President, is that the best option is to wait until the *Iwo Jima* arrives with sufficient helicopter transport and combat marine support to safely extract the marines. We just don't know if the Khmer Rouge will give us enough time to do that. Our backup plan is to use the *Peckham* first for transport, as they have a LAMPS helicopter available and enough gigs to transport the marines to the *Peckham*. If needed, the LFDT is there to provide combat support and rescue of any wounded. I know it's not a great plan, but it's all we have for the next five days."

The president turned to Admiral Humphreys and, with as much calmness as he could muster, stated slowly and succinctly, "Here is what I want: I want those marines off the island with as much speed as humanly possible. I want *nobody* but the people involved to know about it, and I don't want a word in the press about this. This should not have happened and frankly will not happen publicly. After seeing three marines publicly executed by the Khmer Rouge last month, the American voters will have my neck if they see more marines killed or executed. The public will consider this a grave breach of the trust they have placed in us, and after being lied to for the last twenty

years, I don't believe the American public will tolerate the discovery
of yet another lie. I don't care which option you use as long as we
recover those marines, and nobody knows we ever did it. Do I make
myself clear?"

Admiral Humphreys simply said, "Yes, Mr. President. Crystal
clear."

16

LIFE IS WHAT HAPPENS WHILE YOU'RE BUSY MAKING PLANS

A t 0700, the usual announcement came over the *Peckham*'s PA: "Reveille, reveille, all hands heave to and trice up. Prepare for the new day. Sweepers, sweepers, man your brooms. The smoking lamp is now lit in berthing quarters." This was the signal each and every day at sea for the ship's day to start, which was something of an anomaly, considering that watches were still standing, engineers were still making the engines run, radarmen and sonarmen were monitoring their electronic equipment, navigators and boatswain's mates were guiding the ship, and radiomen were on watch. But for the rest of the crew who were not standing watches, it was time to begin the day. Unusually, following this announcement came another: "Landing Force Deployment Team, meet in the CIC at 0730. This is an all-team meeting, with no exceptions."

Following this announcement came another. "This is the captain speaking. I know that we have been very busy with the boat people, and you have all performed admirably. I hope you enjoyed your shore leave, and as you know, because Bangkok was taken off our port stops list, we have been headed back to Subic. Unfortunately, we have been asked to make a slight detour on our way, which will necessitate a delay in reaching Subic. This shouldn't be a long delay, but we changed course a couple of hours ago, and you may have noticed that we picked up some speed. More information will be forthcoming."

As the PA went blank, a "What the fuck? Godamn *BOHICABEC* again," came from the direction of Wonder's rack. Although Wonder loved Subic, he loved Bangkok even more and had already been upset that he wasn't heading there. Wonder had spent most of his time educating Bert on Texas Street and the amazing sexual offerings to be had, including shopping for hookers through storefront windows just like department store displays. Bert, in contrast, had been told about the amazing food and a great downtown market where he could buy plenty of exotic tapestries, rugs, and other hand-made knickknacks for his family. He had been excited to see such an exotic place but was fine heading back for Subic because Pattaya Beach had been so wonderful.

Keeping in mind that the all-call for a meeting of the Ducks had preceded the announcement of the "detour," Bert still tried to be optimistic. "It sounds like this is just a temporary delay, Wonder. Hopefully we won't miss much time in Subic."

"Yeah, BOHICA*fucking*BEC, Bert, another fucking drill for the Ducks and no Bangkok for me," was the only response from the direction of Wonder's rack.

Bert quickly dressed and headed to the mess decks for a quick breakfast of powdered eggs, powdered milk, some sort of meat-like substance, and a piece of toast with imitation peanut butter on it. "Breakfast of champions," he sarcastically said to Scooter, who was in line behind him. Toad, who was behind Scooter, looked at the breakfast as though it was eggs Benedict. All three ate quickly and headed to the Combat Information Center for their meeting. The CIC was a room that Bert always enjoyed seeing. To Bert, it looked like the bridge of the Starship *Enterprise*, with two seats looking much like the captain's seat on a platform above the rest of the equipment, surrounded by techno-geeks who ran the radar and SOs who ran the sonar, sitting at screens with headphones on and a series of lighted glass windows in the middle of the room. As information came in to the electronics technicians and sonar operators, other crew members with wax pencils wrote this information on the lighted windows in different colors so that the captain or whoever was in control of CIC could see. These windows replaced what in Bert's mind should have been that big TV screen that was on the Starship *Enterprise*'s bridge.

As Bert, Scooter, and Toad entered the CIC, they could see that the room, normally abuzz with sailors, was empty apart from the captain, XO, LT Hoffelmeyer, and LTJG Hudson, along with the rest of the Ducks. The officers had incredibly serious looks on their faces, and once the entire team had assembled, Captain Stilton sat in his Captain Kirk seat and addressed the group. "Now, I don't want anyone to overreact, as we don't think we will be called upon to do anything but act as backup. It is critical that you know the information that I am about to give you is top secret and is not to be shared with anyone outside of this room, *and I mean anyone*." Having been a radioman in the navy meant that Bert was well-versed in the whole hierarchy of secrets within the military. Radiomen have the highest security clearances on the ship except for the captain and executive officer, and they routinely handled information that was deemed to be "top secret." When Bert was attending Radioman "A" school, he had to apply for such a clearance, and following his being recruited to the Ducks, he was given a second screening for an even higher clearance, the "Top Secret NATO-SEATO" clearance, which meant that two FBI agents were dispatched to his hometown to interview former teachers, neighbors, and friends about Bert. In fact, Bert had talked to Mike Goldberg, his best buddy in high school, who thought Bert was in big trouble when two FBI agents showed up at his door.

"Don't worry, buddy," Bert remembered Mike saying on the phone. "I didn't tell them anything!"

Bert had told Mike that was exactly the opposite of what he should have done but really couldn't recall having done anything in the small town of Los Alamos that might even remotely disqualify him from such a clearance. Following his second clearance, he clearly recalled the NIS officers who "debriefed" him, telling him all the horrible things the government would do to him if he revealed any top-secret information. Truthfully, during his entire time as a radioman, Bert couldn't recall seeing anything that anyone else would be interested in knowing. Nevertheless, he took seriously Captain Stilton's warning.

"There is a platoon of marines," Stilton continued, "who may need our help. They are on a small island about sixty miles off the mainland of Cambodia, and it seems they are stuck there. It appears that the Cambodians had not been aware of their presence until recently and are now keenly interested in them. The Marine Corps has need of the navy to extract the marines before any serious shit goes down." Stilton paused to let the information sink into the team.

"Now, the USS *Iwo Jima*, a helicopter carrier, is steaming to their aid, but they may be about two days behind us. We are currently about twelve hours from our rendezvous point. The *Iwo Jima* has been tasked with doing the extraction. We are just there for backup. In the event the timing is bad and we need to get the marines off the island before the *Iwo Jima* arrives, we are prepared to use our gigs and the LFDT's inflatables to bring them back here. In that event, you'll be needed for fire support for our crew to protect them on the way in to get the marines. As a final possibility, in the event we are unable to get our gigs to the island due to combat, we will be depending upon you to do the fire support and extraction yourselves. I don't think that's going to happen, so don't get overly worried. It's looking right now like the *Iwo Jima* will be able to handle this with our ship simply lending fire support, which means using our five-inch guns, our BPPDMS missiles and torpedoes if we are required to do so. If there are no further questions, I'll turn things over to LT Hoffelmeyer to coordinate getting you and your equipment ready today, in the event we are needed. Once again, not a word to *anyone*. If they ask why you are preparing, you say it's just an 'exercise.' If there are no questions, then I'll turn the meeting over to LT Hoffelmeyer."

The captain stood, Hoffelmeyer shouted, "*Attention on deck!*" and Captain Stilton left the room.

"I think the captain has given you as much as you need to know for now," LT Hoffelmeyer said. It was obvious to Bert that the LT was attempting to be calm, cool, and collected before his men and knew more than he was letting on. "Go suit up, and we'll meet back up in thirty minutes at the gun locker to start getting equipment ready."

"Holy shit!" Scooter said as they were leaving. "This is real!"

"Guys," Toad said with a look of dismay, "I didn't think we were ever going to have to actually do anything."

Suiting up meant putting on his camos, his web belt with his magazines and his M1911 forty-five caliber pistol, his flak jacket and his additional ammo magazines, and his radio (at sixty pounds) and grabbing his M21 rifle. He felt like a stuffed panda at a carnival and moved much like one also.

Bert's mind, spinning, had to agree with Scooter and Toad. This seemed pretty damn real, he didn't think he'd ever actually be called upon to use any of the information or skills that had passed by them over the last couple of months, and he was, once again, only slightly wishing he had decided to forego being punished for his denture retrieving. At least he would be safely behind bars right now.

17

A NEW DEFINITION OF "SHITSTORM"

As Captain Stilton was meeting with his ship's LFDT, the Cambodians were proceeding to mount an all-out invasion of Squid Island. Two hundred Khmer Rouge troops on ten swift boats and three helicopters were within minutes of the island. As Manny thought about the impending attack, his political scientist hat went on. It was pretty much a sure thing that the Khmer's focus was first and foremost to take as many prisoners as possible and keep casualties as low as possible. From everything Manny read, the Khmer Communist Party wanted as much publicity as possible, and this event would give them the opportunity both for hostages and for more public executions. In proof of Manny's assessment, the Khmer forces were approaching the island slowly, testing the metal of the occupiers. Manny knew that Khmer intelligence was rudimentary at best, but based upon photographs they had surely taken from the helicopter overflights, they would know there was a force of about fifty to sixty men, armed, who were probably combat-trained. Manny hoped that this was just about all that they knew, which would be of benefit to the marines.

Manny had been keeping Corporal Jess Martin, the platoon's

radio operator, very busy. The marines were equipped with two radios on the island. The workhorse was what the military called the AN/PRC-77, or what the navy radiomen and marine radio operators called a "manpack," which was worn on the radio operator's back just like a backpack. The radio was a portable VHF/FM combat-net radio transceiver with over fifty channels and was primarily used in the field to provide short-range, two-way radio. The radio had been stock-and-barrel the most important communications device in Vietnam. It had an encryption system so that the enemy could not listen in but was also only useful to a distance of about five miles.

This was the radio the marines used to communicate with one another on the island but was not useful for long-distance communication. For longer communication, the marines had a US Navy URC-32 transceiver. It contained an ingenious antenna system that could be launched by a large box kite to a height of thirty to fifty feet, in order to provide longer-distance HF and UHF communications. This very crude but ingenious method of creating a tall antenna was enough for the marines to communicate distances far enough to inform command of their situation and was what Corporal Martin was doing nonstop.

Bert had been trained on both radios in "A" school and remembered thanking Ben Franklin for providing the inspiration for such a device. The *Peckham* carried an additional URC-32 in its emergency radio room, a one-man radio shack that was on the ship to be used in the event the main radio shack was destroyed by enemy fire. He had flown the kite several times in drills and was amazed at how well it worked.

Once the *Peckham* was within radio distance of Squid Island, the radiomen on the ship began communicating with the marines, relaying information on to the command via their large, long-distance transceivers. Once the equipment was set up, there was no need for intervention of the shipboard radiomen as the marines' messages were automatically channeled back to command. With this, the radiomen were told only to intervene if there was a problem. The radiomen had the ability to patch both voice and teletype communications to the CIC, where the captain was directing the operation.

The messages from the marines were growing far past urgent. It was obvious that some sort of attack would be forthcoming; however, it was a bit mystifying that the Khmer were not landing or shooting from their sea positions. This made command even more nervous that the Khmer forces would attempt a capture raid rather than a maximum-casualty-producing assault.

The navy command intentionally put the *Peckham* eight nautical miles from Squid Island and on the far west side of the island, away from the Khmer forces. There were two purposes for this. At this distance, the *Peckham* was just over the horizon, so she was not visible to forces on the ground or water. Additionally, the *Peckham* was equipped with a five-inch, fifty-four-caliber Mark 42 gun on the forecastle of the ship, capable of firing forty rounds per minute at a range of eight to twelve miles. The *Peckham* was in a perfect place to provide artillery support to the marines, unseen, and without most of the crew of the *Peckham* seeing what was being fired upon. With the Khmer forces having nothing but a few helicopters and swift boats, there was little danger of any return fire. This, however, was only a complete fallback plan. At the moment, the crew of the *Peckham* had been informed they were on a "training mission," and only the senior officers of the ship and the Ducks knew this was *far* from a drill. Bert, along with everyone else from the president to the marines on Squid Island was hoping the *Iwo Jima* would arrive in time to put down any attack and, he hoped, extract the marines prior to any such attack.

Bert and the other Ducks tried to focus on preparing the boats and the arms and not on being called upon to use them. Bert could not remember a time in his life that he was more anxious. He worked hard to muster up bravado yet sensed that perhaps he was not the only one who felt this way. There was an overwhelming sense that, considering the minimal training they had had and the minimal opportunity to practice their token skills, if they were called upon to provide support to the marines, they would be of little or no help.

As the *Peckham* arrived at its station at approximately 0500 in the morning, the ship's radiomen contacted the marines and patched all communications through to the CIC. Manny took a deep breath as he realized that his platoon was no longer alone in what was shaping up to be a real fight. Captain Stilton explained to Manny the current plan. The *Iwo Jima* was still approximately four to six hours from arriving on station, and its large contingent of UH1 Huey Cobras and CH46 helicopters were still at least two hours out of range. Everyone agreed that it would be best to have the *Iwo Jima* in place, or at least close enough to send in marine reinforcements by helicopter, but everything hinged on what the Khmer did.

The Ducks were busy preparing the inflatable boats for deployment. Along with first-aid equipment, they packed the full small arms array of weapons available to the team. Bert tested his PRC-77 manpack radio, packed extra batteries, and loaded it carefully into his boat.

Although not usually carried on a naval ship, because of the LFDT, each team member had an M16 rifle, the "workhorse" of the Vietnam era. In addition, the Ducks had two thirty-caliber M60 machine guns and four M79 grenade launchers, nicknamed the "blooper," which fired a forty-millimeter grenade. Finally, each of the Ducks carried a Colt forty-five pistol, a tradition on navy ships.

Captain Stilton was on the horn with the *Iwo Jima* and received an update from the captain that at the moment, their maximum-range helicopters were still too far out to dispatch from the ship. Even if they could provide fire support, without the *Iwo Jima* within proximity, there was no place to take the marines, other than airlifting them to the helicopter deck of the *Peckham*, which was only fitted for a small LAMPS helicopter. If the *Iwo*'s helicopters were out of range of the ship, they would have rig for the marines to rappel out of the helicopters and onto the *Peckham*'s helo deck, which would take time, and the helicopters could run out of fuel before they could reach the *Iwo Jima*. As it was, if the Khmer attacked within the next couple of hours, it would be critical for the *Peckham* to extract the marines.

Captain Stilton sent down orders to launch the ship's gigs, which were solid-body boats with inboard engines, and tie them to the *Peckham* to be sure they were ready to go. As he was finishing his discussion with the captain of the *Iwo Jima*, CINPACFLT sent a "flash" message to the *Peckham* that they would need to launch the gigs to extract the marines prior to the Khmer attack. The *Iwo* was simply too far away to handle the extraction. It appeared to the marines that while the Khmer had not yet fired a shot, they were moving closer at a rapid rate of speed, and it now seemed the attack was imminent.

Stilton gave the order to go. He put two Ducks on the captain's gig, one with an M16 and one with an M60 machine gun, launched the inflatables to accompany the gigs to the island, and within minutes, they shoved off. Bert was on an inflatable with the radio, and they arranged two of the inflatables in front of the gigs and two to the sides. Although the twelve-foot inflatables were each equipped with a one-hundred-horsepower outboard engine and were capable of up to about forty knots on good seas, they were limited by the speed of the gigs, which, although well-powered, were not capable of that speed. It was expected that they could reach the island within thirty minutes with current sea conditions. The open sea's waves beat the small inflatables, sending spray crashing into the boats while they were stationary. Bert thought it ironic that he should be this wet, surrounded by ocean, and yet his mouth was as dry as if he had been in the desert. As they set off, this was still *just* an extraction mission, and Bert was in constant contact with the ship, communicating positions and conditions. Even so, he was utterly nauseous and found it difficult to control the shaking in his hands and legs. As he looked around, he saw that he was not alone in his feelings. Scooter looked like he was going to pass out, and Toad was moving his lips. *Was he praying?* Bert wondered to himself. Toad was mindlessly taking out his magazines, one by one, checking the ammo, and replacing them, over and over, in a nervous frenzy. The tension was palpable among each and every person onboard the boats.

The armada was about ten minutes out from the ships when the worst possible news came in. The marines were under fire.

18

WORST-CASE SCENARIO

The first bursts of enemy fire, while not unexpected, stunned Manny like a shovel over the head. As he looked at the ocean from his vantage point, he could see the smoke and flashes from the mounted machine guns on the bows of each of the Khmer swift boats. Manny assumed that the first intention of the Khmer was to push the marines away from any potential landing zone for the boats to make landfall. Immediately, the marines began returning fire until Huck ordered them to cease. The boats were still out of range of the Marines' M16s, and they would be of no use. Manny told Huck to order the marine snipers to take aim, as their range was much greater. He knew from experience that this would have limited effect, simply because the swift boats were bobbing on the sea and thus a difficult target, even for a sniper. Nevertheless, he wanted the Khmer to know that the marines were going to do their best to present a formidable defense of the island.

The marines' knowledge that they were being fired upon by the Khmer was the ultimate confirmation that they were facing a veritable tsunami heading their direction. The marines' preparation included machine gun nests and fortifications, mortars and grenade launchers, sniper scouts, and grenades, and Manny wanted the

Khmer to know that they were *not* going to allow them to penetrate the beach easily. As the swift boats came within range, Manny gave Huck the order to engage, and they began returning fire with all they had. Manny did not know what psychological impact this would have on the Khmer, if any, but he wanted them, in no uncertain terms, to understand that they were *not* facing a naïve or unprepared combat force. The marines' MI6's were on fully automatic, as they had more than sufficient stockpiles of ammunition. The beach, in just a matter of minutes had gone from the gentle sounds of the waves washing up to a confusion of cracks, bangs, explosions, and screams. Manny's intention was to give the Khmer doubt as to the potential success of their attack and hopefully buy time for the helicopters from the *Iwo Jima* to arrive and get them the hell off that island. As the scent of tropical trees and ocean salt was displaced by the acrid smell of gunpowder, Manny watched for any sign that the strike on the Khmer was having an effect. While it was difficult to discern, he sensed that perhaps the level of intensity of return fire was having an influence. Initially, Manny's observers spotted five swift boats, and as the attack continued, three more had appeared. Each swift boat appeared to have fifteen to twenty Khmer soldiers onboard, which meant that the marines were probably outnumbered two to one.

Three swift boats had already made it to the island's shore. As each boat landed, the Khmer poured over the sides as quickly as possible, randomly shooting their weapons in the general vicinity of the marines, in order to provide a bit of cover. Huck, knowing that this was the point at which each individual soldier was most vulnerable, was encouraging the men to capitalize on this momentary weakness and was directing his marines to keep their weapons hot and firing. As the Khmer dashed up the beach toward the marines, Manny watched intently in order to get a better idea of the numbers on each boat as the Khmer did their best to move to cover quickly. From his position on the firing line, it appeared to Manny that the number of Khmer coming ashore was diminishing just a bit. There were still two swift boats he could see that had not attempted to land but seemed to be lingering offshore.

With all of the noise, it was difficult for his sergeants to hear him screaming commands. Fortunately, Manny had been in combat with his sergeants before, and through body language, hand gestures, and bellowing, they understood completely. He yelled at Corporal Martin to radio the *Peckham* that they were taking heavy fire. As he turned to where Martin had been just a moment before, Manny saw him on the ground, having taken a round in the middle of his chest. Martin was dead. Manny called for their corpsman, HM1 Calderone, knowing it would not be of help to Martin, but as he looked around for the corpsman, he saw him feverishly attending to two marines at the same time. One, Corporal Chesney, appeared to be conscious and not seriously wounded. He couldn't see the other marine, but from the look on the corpsman's face, there wasn't much hope for saving him. As Manny was about to grab the radio, another marine pulled it off the back of Corporal Martin and, not knowing what to do, offered the microphone to Manny. Manny grabbed the microphone, pushed the transmit button, and hurriedly informed the *Peckham* of their circumstances, that they were taking heavy fire and things did not look good without some swift help.

As Captain Stilton received the news from the marines, he sent a message to the Ducks that the marines were under fire. He responded to Manny that he was deploying a landing team as quickly as humanly possible and to hang tough. As the team was only ten minutes out from the ship, Stilton decided to order the gigs to stop, for the Ducks to move from the gigs to the inflatables, and to continue to the island at best speed while the gigs returned. A stunned Bert relayed the info to LT Hoffelmeyer. The lieutenant stared at Bert for a split second with what was obvious to Bert as an

"Oh shit" look. Hoffelmeyer took a deep breath, turned to Bert, and told him to call the gigs to come to a full stop and to gather for transfers.

The Ducks had placed an M60 machine gun on the forecastle of each of the gigs, and those important weapons, along with the ammunition, needed to be transferred to the inflatables. Within a few minutes, the team had completely reboarded the inflatables and were now heading to Squid Island, this time at full speed. Bert looked back as he saw the gigs quickly disappearing back toward the ship. He had never felt such a sense of isolation and fear in his life. Scooter threw up over the side of the boat, and Bert was afraid he might join him. As panic pushed its ugly head into Bert's brain, he momentarily lost track of what was going on around him. A surreal sense of doom hit him headlong. *Shake it off, Bert, shake it off,* some part of him was telling his brain and his body. Fortunately, after a few moments, he gathered himself as best he could, and with the tasks before them that they had to do very quickly, he jumped into the moment, which helped him calm down, if just a bit.

LT Hoffelmeyer and the team commanders had determined in advance that if this final and unwelcome scenario became the only choice, the team would proceed to land just south of the southern cove of the island. The assumption was that the Khmer would be using the western cove to alight, and if the Ducks could intercept the Khmer at a perpendicular angle, the marines would be able to face the enemy head-on, while the Ducks could split the focus of the Khmer at their flank, giving the marines the opportunity to inflict greater losses on the enemy by splitting their attention. Now the trick was for this group of completely unprepared, untested, undertrained sailors to do something that the most elite fighting forces would find challenging. Bert would have had to admit the odds were *not* in their favor.

Huck saw Manny struggling with the radio and grabbed another marine to take over for Corporal Martin. Manny let Huck know that help was on the way. What kind of help, he did not know, but the realization that they were not alone gave Manny a moment to feel like he could breathe again. The news that the *Peckham* had a combat team aboard that was heading in their direction gave him greater hope that the marines could persist. It was a moment of anticipation for Manny that perhaps the *Peckham* was carrying a SEAL team with them. It was a very good thing that he didn't know who was coming to support them.

As the Ducks approached within the last mile, they could hear the disquieting sounds of battle clearly. The constant sound of the M16s punctuated by the explosions of chest-throbbing grenades and mortars was terrifying. Tall flumes of smoke and sand rose into the air, and even at a half mile out, the extent of the melee was apparent.

Simultaneously with the Ducks' arrival, two Khmer helicopters appeared in the air racing toward the island and began strafing the marine positions with their door rail guns. It was a bit of good fortune that the Khmer helicopters were not heavily armed. They had not been built as fighter aircraft. Door guns had been improvised on the airships, and it was apparent there were no missiles onboard. Even so, the Khmer were exacting damage on the marine position just because of their positions in the air above them, and Manny knew that that it would not take long for the helicopters to tip the balance in the Khmer's favor.

Even though the Khmer aircraft were not well-armed, the marines *were* equipped to answer their onslaught. Manny's platoon had two shoulder-mounted M67 rifles, and Manny intended for the marines to use them. While these weapons were designed and used as mostly antitank weapons, a skilled operator could use them on slower helicopters. The M67 was a 3.5-inch recoilless rifle and looked much like its prior counterpart, the bazooka. It could also be used against enemy troops themselves with a special round. The weapon was designed to be fired primarily from the ground using the bipod and monopod but could also be fired from the shoulder using the folded bipod as a shoulder rest and the monopod as a front grip. Fortunately for the marines, Manny had two crack M67 operators, and he was counting on them to use the M67 in a way that the engineers of the weapon had *not* designed it for: against the approaching helicopters. On the second pass of the helicopters, Manny gave the signal to fire on them. One was immediately hit, plunging into the shoreline and into a group of Khmer troops. Manny heard whoops and rebel yells from his men, which, even in the midst of such calamity, gave him cause for a quick smile. The small victory gave the marines a boost in momentum and Manny encouragement that maybe there was somebody up above, looking out for them. Manny glanced down at his watch. It was 0714. *Where in the hell are the SEALS from the* Peckham? *How long will it take for the* Iwo Jima's *helicopters to arrive?* To Manny, it was taking far too long for both, and he feared the brutal Khmer had much more to give.

As the Ducks' inflatables closed in on the beach, the anxiety in each sailor increased with each second. At the same time, because they could see the onslaught happening to the marines, their own desire to assist increased also. As the Ducks approached the beach, they still could not see what was happening on the ground, but the sounds of automatic gunfire, grenades, and mortars were a clear confirmation that an all-out assault was in process. The shore waves were light, and a memory flashed through Bert's mind of lying on that white beach in Thailand just days before, looking out at warm blue water, sipping a fancy rum drink. *Ironic*, was all Bert could think, *a place of such peace can be a place of such horrible catastrophe.* As the thought vanished as quickly as it had come, adrenaline coursed through Bert's veins, and his heart felt as though at any moment, it would punch out of his chest. Although the ocean wind had been cool as they screamed toward the beach, Bert was drenched in sweat, so much so that he had to incessantly wipe his eyes.

As the inflatables' engines came to a stop, the moment had come to disembark and move, on foot, to the beach. *No, no, stay! Don't go! You are going to die!* Through some foreign, almost mystical force inside of him, Bert willed his legs to stand, willed his body to move, and willed his arms to grab his rifle against all forms of common sense with which he had been raised, against all means of self-preservation that every human contains inside. It defied logic. It defied intelligence. It is an ironic, uncommon action that men and women have taken many, many times throughout history. It is an act of courage, yes, but it is also an act of humanity, that someone would willingly move *toward* danger and almost certain death, for the benefit of others. It makes no sense, and yet, it makes all the sense in the world.

As the Ducks hurdled from the inflatables into two or three feet of water to run the final few hundred yards or so toward their point of establishment, Bert could feel the warm temperature of the tropical water wash over him, while at the same time his legs felt like rubber, to the point that he wasn't sure he was going to be able to run. Carrying a sixty-pound radio on his back, twenty pounds of ammunition, and his M21 sniper rifle, he could have easily been carrying a boulder on his back. Tripping, he fell face-first into the soft warm beach sand and simultaneously rubbed the sand out of his eyes, while struggling to regain his footing to continue running. When he saw Toad in a similar situation, it was enough of a distraction that he started focusing on him and once again found his legs.

The beach was a small spit of white sand, and just beyond were trees and bushes, hiding the frenzied fighting on the other side of the shrubbery. The deafening sounds of war were overwhelming. Added to this was the buzz inside Bert's brain, which was trying with complete futility to make some sense of the uproar.

The team, now completely unloaded and running full speed ahead, advanced the few hundred feet to their staging point without being seen by the Khmer. Until they reached their assigned position, the team was, likewise, unable to see the Khmer forces. They could still only hear the battle and the earth and smoke being tossed in the air, but now they were close enough to smell the acrid burning scent of gunpowder, the burning jungle, and one another's odor of fear. The Ducks could hear the screams of the warriors on both sides and the cries of what they could only assume were wounded. As they arrived at the staging point, they could clearly see the marines to the left of them and the Khmer at the edge of the cove, to the right. The smells of battle were now heightened by the smells of young men involuntarily releasing their bowels, and the scent of fear became oppressive. Bert knew then that he would never forget the distinctive scent of combat that morning, as well of the smell of fear and even death. As he was orienting himself and preparing to enter the firefight, the battle appeared surreal. Bert watched as he saw both marines and Khmer troops hit by bullets and shrapnel. The team's collective perception was completely unprepared for the magnitude of the bedlam before their eyes. Several times during training, experienced instructors would tell Bert that if he was ever in the middle of combat, things would slow down, and the battle would take place like any of the World War II movies he had watched as a child, with everything happening almost in slow-motion. Exactly the opposite happened for Bert. Everything was happening at once, in lightning speed. For Bert, it was a scene of absolute pandemonium. His eyes were unable to capture the entire landscape. He looked at his fellow team members with both fear and determination in their eyes. He looked toward the fighting, seeing rifles firing on automatic, mortars exploding, and a level of chaos that was impossible for his brain to absorb. It was only when Bert forced himself to view the portions of the battle that he needed to distinguish that he was able to formulate instructions to his limbs to obey.

The moment that Bert realized the Khmer had spotted them and were now aiming in their direction, the survival instinct took over. The fight-or-flight switch in his brain switched to "fight." At least half of the Khmer turned to the side upon realization that they had an additional front and began firing toward the Ducks in earnest. Toad was on the ground next to Bert, already aiming his rifle in the direction of the Khmer. Bert turned to Toad and shouted, "They are fir—"

Before the word *firing* could be completed, Bert saw the back of Toad's neck explode as a Khmer round hit him just below the chin. It seemed incredibly odd, as Bert saw the round hit Toad before he heard the crack of the bullet. Not only did he see the exact moment Toad was hit, because Bert was so close to him, almost touching his shoulder, but he could actually feel the impact of the round on Toad, so much so that for a split second, Bert thought that he, too, had been hit. Blood flew in every direction with a force and intensity unimagined by Bert. The force of impact threw Toad on the ground with such impact that Toad's saliva hit Bert in the face, along with his blood. In panic, Bert started shouting for the doc. The corpsman had witnessed the shot and was already moving toward Bert and Toad. Bert dropped his weapon and grabbed Toad, screaming for him to hang on, crying and wailing at Toad, knowing that he was already gone.

There was no time to process what had just happened, and fortunately for Bert, his brain was in full-adrenalin-crisis mode. Bert, being the radioman, was always required to stay next to LT Hoffelmeyer. His attention split between monitoring the radio transmissions and acting as a rifleman, all Bert could do was return fire, acting as best he could to aim his weapon somewhere in the direction of the enemy. The eleven-pound rifle felt to Bert as though it weighed a hundred pounds, and his manpack radio another hundred, but he simply took a long breath to try to stop what he was sure was hyperventilating and did his best to make sure the muzzle of his rifle was trained somewhere close to the right direction. Taking the time to aim became a ludicrous idea. Just pulling the trigger and hoping the rounds were heading in the right direction was absolutely the most Bert could muster—ironic for one of the team's two snipers.

The Ducks and the marines were throwing grenades at one another much like children in a snowball fight. Fortunately, it looked to Bert like there were no more than a hundred Khmer soldiers on the ground, but they seemed exceedingly close to Bert, so close that he could see their facial features and their uniform insignias and he could hear their shouts. Bert took the time to look out of the cover to the ocean nearby, and with shock and dismay, he could see that there were perhaps eight more boats capable of landing. That guess at a hundred soldiers looked as though it would double within minutes, and it seemed that it would only be a matter of time before the Khmer's sheer numbers would overwhelm both the marines and their new allies, the Ducks. Bert watched with horror as another marine collapsed in a spray of blood and organs. About fifteen feet down the firing line, another Duck took a round in the chest. He wasn't sure who it was but thought that it must have been one of the gunner's mates.

An inescapable sense of doom and a growing conviction that the battle was quickly becoming grave was increasing in Bert's chest. Nevertheless, almost like a machine, Bert was firing, emptying magazines, reloading, and firing again. By the third mag, Bert's brain began thinking again. He slowed the rate of his shots and spent more time aiming and less time simply reacting. From Bert's vantage point, he could not tell who had the upper hand in this fight, but from his completely amateurish vista, things did *not* look great. He was seeing, however, that the addition of the Ducks to fight on the Khmer's flanks had indeed split them, which was giving the marines an opportunity, which he hoped might make the difference.

And then, suddenly, *everything* changed. The rounds from the *Peckham*'s big gun began landing in the harbor in the proximity of the Khmer swift boats that had not yet landed. Because the Khmer forces had not seen the navy warship because of its distance from the island, they must have thought that artillery support would not be forthcoming for the marines. After the first four or five rounds of five-inch shells landed in the cove, the Khmer soldiers gradually decreased the rate of their firing, and it appeared to Bert that they were looking to their field commanders for direction. The possibility came to Bert's mind that the order had been given by the Khmer commanders to retreat. It was obvious that the Khmer were beginning to understand that a US warship was now providing support.

As a fragment of hope began welling up inside Bert and the rest of the team, it was just as quickly dashed. More Khmer helicopters were approaching. Bert could see three or four Khmer helicopters racing for the island with their waist guns blazing. This felt like an attack that couldn't be stopped. Bert could see the marines preparing more M67 rounds and aiming their rifles toward the approaching helicopters, firing as quickly as their hands and their rifles would maneuver. Both M67 rounds missed their intended targets. The automatic fire from the machine guns and M16s did not appear to be slowing the approach of the helicopters, and as quickly as hope had come, the feeling was replaced by confusion and grief.

Yet, once again, a roller coaster of emotions was bolstered. In a surreal sight, it was almost as though the Khmer helicopters had hit some kind of unseen force field. As they approached the island, all three suddenly veered north and then back east in the direction of the mainland. A stunned team stared at what one minute ago had promised to be a slaughter. Now, with a sudden and unexpected change, the threat was moving away from them. It only took a few seconds for Bert to realize the reason behind the sudden turn of fortune. From the west, at least a dozen, and perhaps more, US Marine helicopters led by five UH-1 Huey Cobras blasted over the jungle canopy, just above the trees, with Gatling guns blazing. The *Iwo Jima's* helicopters had made it! In an instant, a simultaneous sense of elation hit marines and Ducks alike, and this time, just like in the movies, the cavalry had arrived at exactly the right time. Two minutes later, and the Khmer would have slaughtered the pinned-down Americans. In an instant, the Khmer headed for open sea faster than a toupee in a hurricane.

The Cobras continued to fire upon the Khmer boats until the last swift boat headed for the safety of the open ocean, then each of the flying gunships climbed to a level of a couple hundred feet and formed a circle around the troops below with their noses all turned outward in a protective pattern. Moments later, a second wave of three CH46 transport helicopters roared in. This time the noise was welcome. Cheers sounded from the Americans on the ground. The helicopters quickly landed on the beach, each with more marines. The escape window probably would not be long, so while the new marines provided potential cover, the beleaguered troops gathered the wounded, the dead, equipment, and weapons and climbed aboard the CH46s.

LT Hoffelmeyer jumped in the helicopter behind LT Manny Kirschoff and smacked him on the shoulder as the helicopters took off, introducing himself to Manny. Manny turned to LT Hoffelmeyer. "SEALs?" he exclaimed.

"Ducks," LT Hoffelmeyer declared with a look of pride, which produced an unfathomable expression of puzzlement on Manny's face.

19

MAKING "THIS LITTLE INCIDENT"
GO AWAY

A s the helicopter gunships patrolled above, two more CH46s landed, each with more marines, who gathered what military paraphernalia they could in less than five minutes. The Ducks' mission was over. For the first time since Toad was hit in that first minute on the beach, Bert looked to his side at the men he had been fighting with. No longer wearing his radio manpack, he glanced at his watch. The time was 0808. The entire event, from landing on the beach to taking off in the helicopter had lasted a little more than forty-five minutes—the longest forty-five minutes Bert would ever spend in his life. As he sat next to LT Hoffelmeyer, he relayed their situation to the *Peckham* and indicated they would be heading to the *Iwo Jima* and from there could be shuttled back to the *Peckham*. Both ships had changed course away from Cambodia and into safer waters. It was only now that the threat was over that the sight of Toad being hit by the round in the neck hit Bert's mind like it did the first time. A sudden grip of guilt hit Bert. Was Toad alive? If so, where was he? What did the doc do? This would be the first of a thousand times that scene would be replayed in his mind.

Doc came rushing up to Bert, saying, "Are you shot?"

Bert looked at Doc questioningly and then looked at the side of his uniform, once green camouflage, now blood-soaked. Bert realized it was Toad's blood on him. "I'm fine," Bert mumbled, suddenly feeling like he was going to vomit. Knowing what the answer was, Bert asked, "Is Toad going to be okay?"

When Doc just shook his head, no more words needed to be exchanged. Toad was dead. Dead. *How can something like this happen to such a kind person? Where is any justice in all of this?*

Bert fought back the urge to wretch, as there were still tasks to be accomplished. LT Hoffelmeyer told Bert to relay to the *Peckham* that they had two casualties and that he believed the marines had lost four men. As Bert relayed this information, his voice faltered several times. Feeling the surreal becoming real to him as his racing mind gradually slowed to a pace where he could think rationally again, his brain kept repeating the message he had just conveyed. *Six deaths.*

"I know it doesn't sound right to say it," Manny said to LT Hoffelmeyer, "but I'm grateful the losses were as small as they were. When I saw the number of those assholes hitting the beach, I couldn't imagine a scenario in which we would survive. I lost four men who had all made it through two tours in-country. The war was supposed to be over. We were supposed to be done with this. And yet, I guess our record as human beings, if anything, demonstrates that war is never over. Things like this are always going to happen." He shuddered, lamenting at the state of humanity in the world, for just a moment, and then quickly shook it off. Manny looked up at LT Hoffelmeyer. "I have no idea what a 'Duck' is, but your support bought us the time we needed to get our Cobras there. You made a big difference today, and you saved lives."

"I've never been in battle before this," LT Hoffelmeyer said softly, "but hell can't be much different than what we saw today. Thank you for letting me know your assessment of the support we gave today. We're proud to have helped, if just a bit. I'll relay that to my team. If you'll excuse me, Lieutenant, I'm going to go chat with my men," he said, choking up and wiping the tears from his eyes as he walked to the back of the transport.

As LT Hoffelmeyer left, his spot was taken by LTJG Hudson. Bert, completely exhausted, both mentally and physically, thought to himself that he just could not take one more bit of Rock's bullshit and braced himself for the usual bullying. Instead, Rock, who appeared equally wearied, stared at Bert with his usual "you shall have my wrath" look, which immediately changed to a weary smile and offered his hand. "You did good, Bertram," Rock said. He too got up and went to the rear of the helicopter, leaving Bert in stunned disbelief.

The remainder of the ride was completed in silence. Neither the experienced marines nor the inexperienced Ducks could muster much of a conversation. Bert, left to his own thoughts, realized that he wasn't thinking much, at all. It was as though his body was doing the thinking, which might best be described as a bone-weary fatigue, a sadness, and relief, throughout his entire body. The adrenaline had left his system, and the weight of the last couple of hours repressed any analysis. There would be time for that. Right now, he appreciated just not thinking much of anything.

As the helicopters landed on the *Iwo Jima*, the last thing LT Hoffelmeyer said to the Ducks was "People are going to have lots of questions. Not *one* word to anyone from you, other than you were on a training exercise. Period. It doesn't matter whether they believe you or not. That's what you say. Clear?" It was evident that there would be no talk of this, at least not for now.

The Ducks were met by two marines who told them they would escort them to a temporary berthing compartment. As it turned out, it was an empty berthing compartment typically used when they had a full marine detachment onboard. The Ducks had the compartment to themselves, and Bert couldn't help but suspect that they were being isolated from the rest of the crew. Bert assumed that their stay on the *Iwo Jima* would be temporary until they could arrange for a gig to transport them back to the *Peckham*. The marines brought them ditty bags with the basics—soap, shampoo, razors, and toothbrushes —and took estimates of their sizes so they could receive fresh dungarees. LTJG Hudson stopped in and informed the Ducks that they were going to have a team meeting in an hour and to shower, shave, and be there on time. He stopped before leaving and said, much to the shock of the sailors, "You guys did good out there today. You saved lives. You should be proud of yourselves."

An hour later, the Ducks, less Toad and GM2 Benson, the team's two casualties, met in an empty mess close to their berthing compartment. LT Hoffelmeyer praised the group for the courage and effectiveness they showed that morning, and they bowed their heads and prayed for Todesky and Benson and for their families. "I just had the honor of speaking to Admiral Ira Stephens, our Chief of Naval Operations, and General Robert Hastings, Commandant of the Marine Corps. They send their congratulations and their gratefulness at the job we did today. I want to add my praise also. I know it's been a whirlwind since we started this LFDT journey, and we've had a lot of bumps in the road. I know we could have been better prepared and better trained, and, truthfully, I think we all believed that with Vietnam ending, we would not be called on for anything more than drills. But we were called upon, and we rose to the occasion, and LTJG Hudson and I are both very proud to have been given the opportunity to lead you in this.

"I know you are expecting to be transferred back to the *Peckham*," expressed LT Hoffelmeyer, "but the navy has decided that they want you to head back to Subic for detailed 'debriefings' before returning to the *Peckham*. The crew of the *Peckham*, except for those who absolutely needed to know, have been informed you have been on a training exercise. They are resuming their deployment while we head to Subic, and we'll meet up in a couple of weeks. We're about six days out from Subic, so in the meantime, I want you to feel like you have time to rest. There will be no watches; we have our own mess decks so we will share meals together, and we'll do movies on the mess decks tonight. You can get fresh air if the weather allows, but, and I am giving you a direct order, if anyone, and I mean *anyone*, asks about what happened out there, you are to say nothing except that you were on a 'training exercise.' Understood?"

Heads nodded, and "aye aye, sirs" were halfheartedly given. Unknown to the Ducks, the marines from Squid Island were placed in the exact same position, isolated from the rest of the crew and given the same orders. Bert had no idea why they weren't to talk about it, but as a radioman, he knew that the military was all about their little secrets. Every watch he had stood as a radioman, he saw messages marked "Top Secret," and he had been schooled long and hard about the consequences of sharing that information in the wrong places. For the rest of the Ducks, these orders made no sense at all, and because they all had only themselves to talk to about it, they did quite a bit of grumbling and speculating during the six days back to Subic.

The next six days were good and bad. Bert relaxed, was fed more and better food than he had been used to on the *Bob E.*, had a chance to catch up on reading, and sunned himself on the signal bridge of the *Iwo Jima*. It was a time to try to feel like a human being again and to take time to be grateful he had survived. It was also a time of vivid nightmares, randomly reliving the moments of battle, and grief over the loss of Toad. This circle of reliving would carry Bert throughout his life. He would wake with nightmares well into his sixties, and he assumed it was not unlike the experiences of the other Ducks. Just when he thought it was gone, it would rear its ugly head and remind him that it happened.

As it was, he was safe and could relax just a bit. It was a good thing that no alcohol was allowed on navy ships. He might have been tempted to drink away his feelings. As a poor substitute, Bert listened to Willie Nelson sing "Whiskey River" somewhere in the neighborhood of five hundred times during those six days. He was amazed at how many country songs were about drowning your feelings in alcohol. He was beginning to "get" country music in a way he never had before.

Admiral Ira Stephens and General Hastings had several meetings in the next few days after the incident, and the president was briefed on the final action plan. The flag officers were commended by the president for the fact that not one word had reached the press about what he called *this little incident.*

"You know, Ira, that there is no fucking way somebody isn't going to talk about this, right?" said Hastings. "There are just too many actors. We have the line officers on two ships, we have ten helicopter pilots, we have thirty-five marines, seven air force security police officers, and seventeen sailors. You just can't keep that many people quiet about this," Hastings asserted.

"I do agree that there are people who will talk. But if we make sure that the primary people who had eyes on the ground are given an ultimatum and if we can keep the vast majority quiet and if confronted, give public denials about this, then the few who choose to violate their orders will be seen as nuts or conspiracy theorists, and they won't be believed. We humiliated the Khmer, so they have no advantage in going public with this information, and, frankly, we can just deny it. The key will be to ensure that each of the soldiers, sailors, and airmen directly involved are threatened within an inch of their lives of the devastating consequences of going public and that they decide to do the right thing with it."

The Joint Chiefs decided to bring in experts in this area, and there were no better experts than the CIA. Although the CIA had been directly involved in Vietnam since 1954, over the course of the last few years, their contribution became critical. During Vietnam, the CIA built skills sufficient to carry out "high political and psychological impact actions against military targets in North Vietnam," which opened the door wide to power and control in Southeast Asia. One of the things they became masters at was psychological warfare, recruiting psychologists and behavioral scientists to create new methods of collecting intelligence, propagating false information, and undermining the enemy from a psychological perspective. Even in the early 1970s, stories ran rampant of the CIA's complicity in drug trafficking in Laos and the opium trade, with the intention of pacifying as many tribes in Indochina as possible. Now that Vietnam had officially ended, the CIA, which had amassed a huge amount of power in Washington, DC, was struggling to redefine itself. There was going to be at least one more mission for the agents and psychologists in the Agency: making Mūc Ong cease to exist. The CIA dispatched a team to Subic Bay to ensure they were prepared for the arrival of sailors and marines on the *Iwo Jima*, to accomplish just that.

20

GUILT, PATRIOTISM, AND OUTRIGHT THREATS

Three days prior to the arrival of the *Iwo Jima*, seven people landed at Cubi Point Naval Air Station on the grounds of Naval Station Subic Bay. In the early morning hours, a red and white Beechcraft King Air touched down and taxied to an awaiting gray van. The seven people disembarked the airplane and quietly loaded into the van for a small set of buildings just north of the airfield, which contained barracks, administration buildings, and transportation. The buildings were vacant except for a small marine guard. When the van arrived in front of the set of buildings, just as quietly as they arrived, the group disembarked the van and went inside the building to set up their operations.

Three days later, the *Iwo Jima* pulled into Subic Bay and unceremoniously tied up to the pier. Fifty-seven people came down the gangplank wearing identical nondescript dungarees and loaded into five vans, which traveled approximately fifteen minutes to the same building the seven people had entered three days prior. The Ducks and the marines were kept in segregated barracks. They were told to settle in and to plan for about a week's stay. The Ducks were told they would rejoin the *Peckham* when it arrived, and the marines were

slated to fly to Okinawa. They were told that the purpose of this time
was to "debrief" the happenings on Mūc Ong.

The CIA had five days to accomplish one goal with the servicemen: make Mūc Ong disappear. The goal was to be accomplished in
four ways:

1. Scare the shit out of the servicemen with stories of how
   bad it would be for them if they ever spoke about the
   incident.
2. Repeatedly remind them of their oaths and the imperative
   of the security of the United States in this matter and
   convince them that telling anyone anything other than the
   story they were about to learn would put them on a par
   with the greatest traitors in the world, oh, say, Brutus and
   Benedict Arnold.
3. Give them a new story to tell everyone that would be
   consistent among all fifty-seven of the servicemen.
4. Practice that story over and over until the servicemen
   began to believe it themselves.

None of the seven "facilitators" mentioned the CIA or that the CIA
was their employer. They all introduced themselves to the teams as
"Dr." So-and-so or "Mr." This or That. During their first meetings
with the Ducks, they were cordial and very professional.

The day started with individual meetings with each of the Ducks.
Several hours of meetings had already taken place, and Bert had yet
to be called. The remaining Ducks immediately began to speculate
on what was taking place. "Do you remember our SERE training
instruction?" Scooter said to Bert. "All those things they taught us
about resisting interrogation. I think maybe this is going to be some
torture interrogation and that we are being tested again."

"Oh, come on, Scooter," Bert said with an eyeroll. "Our stuff is
done. I think they just want to be sure they understand what

happened out there and to give us a chance to tell our story. These folks are on our side." Bert hoped he was right, but the mystery that surrounded the meetings was disconcerting, to say the least. "I guess we'll just have to see what they have to say and what they want to know."

"Well, I'm going in with the attitude that I'm a POW, and I'm going to use my SERE training from the start," said Scooter, with his chest barreled out. Bert noticed that mild-mannered Scooter had been changed during their mission. He actually believed now that he was a *badass*.

SERE training, which is another military acronym for "survival, evasion, resistance, and escape," had been born out of Vietnam. The military command realized early on that they were going to lose troops to POW camps and that they should prepare them for the possibility. SERE was mandatory training for pilots, special forces, and others most likely to be captured, and the military then created different levels, depending upon the job of the service person. Eventually, everyone got classroom training on SERE, but it was mostly lectures on the code of conduct for POWs and the POW's duty to try to escape. Anyone who went through basic training or boot camp received that first level. The other levels were increasingly sophisticated up to the level "C" training given to all special forces and anyone likely to be shot down over enemy territory, which included actual escape and survival scenarios and a stay at a mock POW camp that looked surprisingly similar to the "Hanoi Hilton" of Vietnam fame. For most attendees, the focus was on resistance to exploitation and political indoctrination and escape planning. Like the other training they received, the Duck version was a highly abbreviated experience at SERE, which translated mostly into the instructors scaring the shit out of them, explaining that if they succumbed to interrogation or allowed themselves to be used as a propaganda tool, things would not go well once they were home. Bert really didn't think he was going to have to apply any of those skills in this context, but the rest of the Ducks were getting quite stirred up about it.

Each time one of the Ducks was brought back from what the

facilitators called "debriefing," Bert found him to look just a bit shaken. They were all very quiet and unwilling to talk much with the others about their experience. While this was a bit unsettling to Bert, nobody had broken bones or open wounds, so he considered that to be a good sign. When Scooter returned, he was behaving exactly like the others. The bravado he'd shown prior to the meeting had evaporated somewhere along the way. Bert had not had a chance to process the sight when a nice-looking woman wearing black glasses opened the door and said kindly, "Seaman Matthew Bertram?" Bert stood, unsure what the next hour would bring.

As they started walking together down the hallway, the woman in black glasses smiled, put out her hand, and said to Bert, "Matthew, I'm Doctor White. How are you doing today?"

"Truthfully, I'm a little nervous, Doctor," Bert replied.

"I completely understand, Matthew. It's quite natural, but I assure you, this will be quite simple and, hopefully, stress-free."

As they opened the door into the debriefing room, Matt noticed a simple table in the middle of the room with one chair on one side, two on the other, and an older man sitting at one of the chairs. He looked around the room for that one-way mirror they always have in police dramas but found only a dull yellow shade of paint on the walls, with no pictures and not much in the way of decorating. Above the man hummed the sound of a fluorescent light, a noise that had always annoyed Bert to an extent. He found the buzzing very distracting. Unfortunately, that appeared to be the only kind of light fixture the navy used, shipboard or on land.

"Matthew, this is Mr. Duncan," Dr. White said as they entered the room.

Mr. Duncan stood, extending his hand, giving a warm smile, and saying, "It's a pleasure to meet you, Seaman Bertram. I understand that your nickname on the ship is Bert, correct?"

Bert nodded, giving a "Yes sir," as he absorbed the fact this this man had personal information that somebody had provided. *These two spooks definitely did their homework.* John le Carré was Bert's favorite author, and his favorite le Carré book was *The Spy Who Came in from the Cold.* He had just finished le Carré's newest book, *Tinker, Tailor, Soldier, Spy* just a few weeks ago, and hence, the main character of the book, George Smiley, was vivid in his mind. Bert was sure these two were "spooks," as he was pretty well educated in this area from the novels he had read over the last couple of years. He decided to approach this whole meeting with a George Smiley kind of attitude, including spy terms like *spook.* As the two spooks were shuffling papers, preparing for the conversation, Bert assessed Mr. Duncan, and as Mr. Duncan spoke, in the back of Bert's mind was le Carré's description of George Smiley: *he looks like a mixture of Humpty-Dumpty and a Cornish elf—very short and broad—and I don't think he's anyone's fool.* After all Bert had seen and done the last couple of days, he didn't think he would ever be shaken by anything again. Bert was definitely getting into the role.

"Seaman Bertram, are you okay?" Mr. Duncan was saying.

As Bert's mind gradually left England and returned to the drab room, Mr. Duncan started over. "I asked if you would be okay with me calling you Bert."

"Certainly, Mr. Duncan," said Bert. "And what may I call you?"

This caused a moment of confusion in Mr. Duncan, and then, with a savage seriousness in his eyes, he replied, "Mr. Duncan will be just fine for now, Bert."

Doctor White continued, "The purpose of our meeting today, Bert, is to provide you with the support you need following what was probably a few quite stressful days. We want to be sure that you have some time to process things prior to going back to your ship. Just a little retreat so that you're not thrown back into things unprepared."

"And also," Mr. Duncan said, "to remind you of your duties and your obligations as a US Navy serviceman."

Ah, here it comes, thought Bert. *The expected hammer.* The drills that the Ducks had received in SERE training suddenly jumped to the forefront of his mind. He recalled at one point having to recite verbatim, the "Navy Code":

. . .

Article I—I am an American, fighting in the forces which guard my country and our way of life. I am prepared to give my life in their defense.

Article II—I will never surrender of my own free will. If in command, I will never surrender the members of my command while they still have the means to resist.

Article III—If I am captured, I will continue to resist by all means available. I will make every effort to escape and to aid others to escape. I will accept neither parole nor special favors from the enemy.

Article IV—If I become a prisoner of war, I will keep faith with my fellow prisoners. I will give no information or take part in any action which might be harmful to my comrades. If I am a senior, I will take command. If not, I will obey the lawful orders of those appointed over me and will back them up in every way.

Article V—When questioned, should I become a prisoner of war, I am required to give name, rank, service number, and date of birth. I will evade answering further questions to the utmost of my ability. I will make no oral or written statements disloyal to my country and its allies or harmful to their cause.

Article VI—I will never forget that I am an American, fighting for freedom, responsible for my actions, and dedicated to the principles which made my country free. I will trust in my God and in the United States of America.

.   .   .

At the time these were committed to memory, Bert saw them as just a chore, to be memorized just like the Nicene Creed in catechism class. Now, Mr. Duncan and Doctor White began to get serious.

"Although we're happy to listen if you have things you want to tell us, we have a pretty good handle on the happenings of the last couple of days."

Happenings? thought Bert. He had heard some mind-bending euphemisms before, but to describe what had happened as a *happening* took them to an all-time level.

"And since we have a good understanding of all of that, we thought we'd talk about your oath as a serviceman and your duty to your country."

Oh shit, Bert thought, *pulling out the flag and dusting off the Pledge of Allegiance. I know the UCMJ will be next.*

"We need you to understand that the Vietnam era is completely over, and the Americans, whom you serve, want to get on with their lives, and they do not want to hear anything more about fighting and especially about servicemen dying on foreign soil right now. The president and the Joint Chiefs of Staff have determined that the happenings of the last few days never happened. You, as a radioman understand the meaning of 'top secret' more than most, and I need to inform you that this carries an even higher standard than top secret."

Bert was unhinging in front of these two spooks. *People died for their country, and we are supposed to completely ignore this?* He searched his head for something he had ever heard of that was higher than top secret. He was simply unable to keep his mouth shut after hearing this. "I guess *super-duper double hex on you top secret* was something they didn't bother to teach me in school. What this means is that as far as the government is concerned, this did not happen? Is that what you are telling me? That's completely ridiculous!" There, it was out.

"It is classified to the point that if you ever divulge these happenings to anyone else, no matter how far in the future this is, you will be prosecuted for treason and will either be shot or spend the rest of your life in a military prison. You will forever be another Benedict Arnold, Bert. Furthermore, none of these events go on your military record, there is no 'history' to be recorded, all paperwork regarding this matter will be destroyed, and no medals or honors will be bestowed. That's your duty to your president and your country, and you will honor that order."

"What do I tell my shipmates when I return, then? How do I explain to them that Todeski and Benson are dead? How do I explain where I've been and what I've done? How can I *plausibly* say any of that? They saw us preparing and leaving the ship. Hell, the *Peckham* fired its guns on the Khmer. You can't just make that go away!" Bert realized he was shouting just at the moment he realized that these were probably two of the worst possible people to shout to.

"We understand that this will be very challenging for you, Bert. And that's why we are here. We are going to help you understand the official story and to give you practice in the next few days, so that by the time you get back to the *Peckham*, you'll believe it yourself. For now, head back to the barracks, relax, and tomorrow we'll work on getting this all straight in your mind. By the way, you also are not allowed to discuss this between yourselves in the barracks. Just so you know, we're keeping an eye on you until you become comfortable with this new way of thinking."

Fucking impossible, Bert thought. He hoped he said that in his mind and not out loud.

Over the next few days, Bert, the ducks, and presumably the marines were all told the story Bert entitled in his mind, "The Story of How Nothing Happened."

For the sailors, it was a training mission that was a joint mission with the Marine Corps and intended to be a realistic test of the Ducks' skills. After the drill, they went back to the *Iwo Jima* so that military command could get their perspectives as LFDT members so that the navy could improve the training. The *Peckham* served as support to lob shells into the bay simply to make the exercise feel more realistic. Unfortunately, there was an accident on one of the inflatables, and two members of the Ducks fell overboard in rough seas and perished. Military members die all the time in "training accidents," and this is a sad but unfortunately realistic risk with these kinds of exercises.

Several of the *Peckham* crew members who knew a little more received some debriefing of their own, on a smaller scale, but it was plausible and was mostly not spoken of again by any member of the Ducks.

Bert and the Ducks headed back to the *Peckham* at the end of the week, and none were quite sure what the real story was. After practicing the new stories a hundred times in that administrative building on the north end of the airfield, doubts began to creep in. The CIA psychologists knew a thing or two about memory. Each time a memory is relived, it changes, and it is possible, perhaps not perfectly, to nurture a new memory in the place of the old one. They were very good at what they did.

21

PERFECTLY NORML

A t the end of the week, the sailors were released but not without a final cautionary tale about traitors and the like from the spooks. Bert had had just about enough yet understood completely that these people were very, very serious.

The *Bob E.* had arrived in Subic, and the rest of his shipmates were enjoying, once again, all that the best liberty port in the area could provide. It was actually amazing, but he was faced with few questions from his friends, who were simply happy to have him back.

One afternoon over a beer in Subic, Wonder turned to Bert. "We heard you were just on an exercise. But we saw some shit from our vantage point that sure didn't look like an exercise. Tell me, Bert. What really went on there?"

Bert smiled and with an ease that amazed him, said, "It really was *just* an exercise, Wonder. Truly."

The carryings-on in Subic were the same, but Bert felt like a different person. Yes, he drank. Yes, he told and listened to the sea stories, many of which involved him at this point. He agreed that he was there when a sea story got out of hand and ended up in the land of that just didn't happen. He would swear on a stack of Bibles that yes, it definitely happened, exactly as it was told.

Bert still had two and half years left on his enlistment. It seemed like such a long time he had been there. He started a calendar with 912 days left until discharge. He had more adventures, drank more beer, and spent time on deployment helping with orphanages, and yet he had lost something very important in his life—his innocence. When the navy approached him about re-enlisting at the end of his hitch, he smiled and simply said, "No."

As Bert grew older, and what was left of his naïveté was sapped, he often reflected upon the sad fact that this "little incident" was not the first time that soldiers had died for a cause that was unrecognized, hidden, and intentionally forgotten and would not be the last. Two sailors and four marines died in unrelated "training accidents," and their heroism and the heroism of the survivors would never be recognized. No shiny shit would be pinned to their uniforms. No history books would record it.

EPILOGUE

In the days, weeks, years, and decades that passed, occasionally, a former Duck, mostly after he had consumed a bit too much alcohol, would tell the story of Mūc Ong and the Ducks to friends, a partner, a spouse, or his children. But in the morning, when he was once again sober, the story, just like so many others, would not be spoken of, and those who had listened to it would chalk it up to an old sailor who was *just* telling a sea story.

ABOUT THE AUTHOR

Mark David Albertson is what some of his friends have called a *Renaissance man*, which in Mark's mind is a great term for someone who couldn't decide what to do in life. Mark grew up in Los Alamos, New Mexico, "The Atomic City." Joining the US Navy after high school, he served at the end of the Vietnam era and mostly in the midst of the Cold War, being discharged honorably (mostly). He enlisted in the Texas Air National Guard during college, serving as a staff sergeant, and attended college at the University of Texas at San Antonio and then law school at St. Mary's University in San Antonio, Texas. Mark practiced law as a prosecuting attorney and in private practice for over thirty years in Washington state before returning to his beloved Texas. Along the way, he owned a private investigation agency and a hypnotherapy practice and pursued other various and random distractions. As an attorney, he was nationally and internationally published in law journals and law books, spoke internationally on legal issues, taught college classes as an adjunct professor, and managed to help with the raising of three fine children. Mark currently lives with his wife, Karen, in the Hill Country of Texas on their ranch, *Los Perros Locos*, and all of the children at home currently have fur and tails. This is Mark's first novel.